VIA FOLIOS 80

SLED RUN

A NOVEL BY
ROSS TALARICO

BORDIGHERA PRESS

Library of Congress Control Number: 2012938386

©2012 by Ross Talarico.

Printed in the United States.

Published by
Bordighera Press
John D. Calandra Italian American Institute
25 West 43rd Street, 17th Floor
New York, NY 10036

VIA Folios 80
ISBN 1-59954-043-6
ISBN 978-1-59954-043-6

To my sisters, Judy (rest her wonderful soul) and Lonnie,
my great companions through life.
And to my children, may their complex lives be
tempered by the love of family.

CONTENTS

PREFACE

9

PART ONE
*
The Warmest Autumn

11

PART TWO
*
Sled Run

91

PART THREE
*
Christmas Morning

143

PREFACE

Under the big wet flakes of this December snowfall, I turn instinctively toward the hazy light of the winter sky, and I hold my hand up over my eyes, squinting not so much as to keep the snow away, but to see back over the years. And sure enough, there's Danny at the top of the small hill at the street corner, waving to me, shouting something with his great laugh and pointing to Cosmo who is leaning with his sled against the dead elm, furiously packing a snowball. It is late afternoon. The light begins to fall, but not our spirits. We breathe in the grey shadows of the neighborhood until the darkness surrounds the glow of our hearts. Cosmo makes another run down the hill, over the sidewalk, down the driveway of Alex the Truckman, and onto the ice-covered street where he glides all the way to the streetlamp in front of my house. And just as Danny grabs his sled to run the same course and push harder for a few more feet, the silhouettes of three men appear on the backside of the hill. It is the older guys, Carm, Johnny, and Bambi, dragging with them the most splendid sled I have ever seen— wide, polished chrome runners, and oak rails so deeply rubbed and oiled the grain looks like pinstriping. Piled on the back of it, what looks like a hundred brightly wrapped packages with glittering gold and silver bows. And it is Carm who gets on at the top of the hill, and he extends his hand my way and invites me to get on that grand sled too. Holding on tightly, careful not to disturb the gifts, we fly down the hill with a grace I have never felt before. Over the driveway, onto the icy street, and then up, up, into the air, past the streetlamp, over the houses on our street and into the night. Carm turns to me and winks, and I feel no fear at all to be floating over my city, the lights flickering below me. "Relax," I hear Carm say as he glides the sled downward, and I feel the strange joy of this, the grandest of sled runs . . .

PART ONE

*

The Warmest Autumn

CHAPTER I

October, 1959

The world seemed to change that warm October morning as I stood at the bus stop at the corner of Bay and Goodman and Carm Carlotta drove up in his new candy-apple red Mercury convertible, top down, chrome spinners on the hubs, continental wheel cover extended a foot beyond the back bumper—and on the radio, rising out of the quadraphonic speakers, Tommy Edwards singing his new hit, *It's All in the Game.*

"Late for school?" Carm asked, his right arm hung on the seat top as if around some invisible girl—and without waiting for an answer, added "Hop in, I'll take ya . . . ."

Two weeks earlier he had let us sit in the Mercury for a few minutes after we waxed it for him at the corner gas station, Jack's Mobil, where we all hung out. Carm would give us ten dollars to split among ourselves along with a six-pack of beer. He'd let us keep whatever was left of the Blue Coral Wax besides, and we'd take it home and use it on our dads' cars—though it wasn't the same feeling shining up a five-year-old, beat-up Plymouth sedan. Carm was in his early twenties, but already he seemed to have leapt over the gap between the neighborhood and the dreams of the neighborhood boys. It seemed just a couple of years earlier he was selling hub-caps out of his mother's thoroughly rusted Chevy's trunk, or sprinkling the half-built frame of the new house on Cummings Street with gasoline before Johnny Pops, the insurance man's son and neighborhood bully, set it ablaze after midnight.

Carm still stopped in and parked at the gas station some nights—as did his younger brother Phil, who was the first kid on the block to become a policeman. Phil would show up once in a while in his uniform, so blue, sparkling, and official; most of us felt pretty good about it, but not Johnny Pops, Phil's best buddy as a kid. Johnny resented it—but then Johnny seemed to resent a lot of things.

You could find Carm any morning, like always at the *Donut Hole* in the shopping plaza. Lots of times he'd buy your coffee and you wouldn't even know until you tried to pay for it. He spent a lot of time at the downtown clubs and, as Cosmo's old man mentioned one night because he worked in the parking lot across the street, Carm was in and out of swank *Eddie's Chop House* at all hours, so he must have been doing okay.

The wind caught the collar of Carm's silky white shirt as he drove down Goodman and then up East Main Street to my school, East High. I was in ninth grade, and yes, I was a little late that day—but not late enough to miss riding past a number of kids who were hoofing it. I lay my head back and, though I had to stretch a little, rested my elbow on the top of the open window. Carm drove slowly, the easy rumble of the dual Hollywood glasspack mufflers just enough to turn the heads of others. Tommy Edwards sang on—*soon I'll be there at your side, with a sweet bouquet* . . . I hoped somehow we'd pass Leona.

Over the bridge on Main Street I caught a glimpse of the high school, and for a moment I imagined Carm would simply pass it up and let me ride with him for awhile. The Mercury seemed to float down the road, the sun pouring over my face in a baptism of movement and sound. I closed my eyes, but Carm asked, "Do you like school?" and I opened them again and sat up a little. By the time I said "Yea, it's okay Carm," he had stopped the car in front of the high school. I tried to take my time getting out, and I looked around a little and sure enough, a lot of guys and girls were looking over at us.

"Thanks Carm . . . see you at the station," I said as he cruised away.

I quickly dissolved into the crowd up the stairs to the entrance as the bell rang. Danny Polito, one of my two best friends (the other was Cosmo Bellavia, both Cummings Street boys), came up behind me and gave me a purposeful shove.

"You sonofabitch," he smiled, "a ride with Carm on a day like this—are your pants wet or what."

I tried to hold back, but I let out a big grin and punched him on the shoulder. "Jesus Danny, what a car—it was like heaven, I mean shit Dan you forget about everything. You know," I paused for a moment at the top of the stairway, "when he pulled up here just now to let me off Dan—with everybody just hangin' out waiting for that lousy bell to ring—I almost asked Carm why he was stoppin'—like where the hell he was bringing me . . . "

"Back to reality, eh Rosey." Danny said, reaching out and touching my forehead, as if to check for a fever. "Study hard Bright Boy," he said sarcastically, "and someday you'll be cruising with the top down and the sky wide open . . . just like California—I hear half the cars are rag-tops there." Danny was always talking about California, about moving there with his dad and his sister.

"Shit," I said, turning down the hallway and heading toward my homeroom.

That morning it was my turn to stand up in front of the homeroom class to collect for the *March for Dimes*. The first dime caught me right in the throat, and I said *fuck* and Mr. Penfield, the homeroom teacher, gave me a dirty look, so I started dodging and dancing under a barrage of coins as the students threw their charitable donations at me. A nickel chipped the paint above the blackboard and Mr. Penfield bellowed keep it down (the coins, not the noise level). We collected almost six bucks that morning, and I got away with two nicks, one behind my ear and another between two fingers on my left hand.

In English class, Mr. Penfield gave us a half-hour to complete the essay. I didn't think I'd have any problem with the essay since the question had been given to us the previous day and I had talked it over with my dad the night before both at supper and before I went to bed. But for the first five minutes I simply stared at the question at the top of the mimeographed hand-out:

What is your vision of an ideal world?

I thought back to my dad's smile when I showed him the question the previous night. "Goddamn, that's easy," he laughed, "plenty of lobster tails and Good + Plenty's."

"Someone to do the dishes," my mother chimed in as she rinsed out a cup in the sink. My older sisters, Lonnie, a senior at East High, and Judy, a junior, stopped arguing about whose turn it was to do the dishes and looked over at me.

"Another dumb question," Judy complained, sounding a bit older than her seventeen years. She was the intellectual among us. "When will teachers learn that when you ask dumb questions, you get dumb answers."

"Teachers . . . learn?" It's beneath them, laughed Lonnie, and my dad laughed with them. Ordinarily my mother would have reminded my sisters to show a little respect—but this was a typical conclusion to our family dinner, ending in either laughter or argument, and many times both. As far as I knew, we were the only family in the neighborhood who had discussions routinely. And my mom loved it, beaming devilishly from her quiet retreat, her dark eyes sparkling, her black hair swept back from her forehead. But then she stepped forward to the center of our tiny kitchen, held a pan she was drying to her waist with one hand and pointing a dishcloth toward my father with the other:

"Sam, Rosey's asking you a serious question—and all you do is joke with your daughters . . . "

To tell the truth, I liked joking more than anything. My dad had a sense of humor—everyone knew that. But there was that serious, mysterious side too. So when he developed an ulcer later on, no one was as surprised as they made out to be. I guess there were some things we'd never know about him—like the books he brought home for our shelves (no other house had as many) that only Judy took the time to read, books with titles like *The Last of the Mohicans, Faust, Crime and Punishment,* by authors whose names I couldn't even pronounce. No, there were some things we'd never understand, like how he didn't cry at the wake of our grandmother, his mom, or our grandpa either . . .

I stared at that question until I heard Mr. Penfield say you *should* be writing. On top of the blank page I wrote the sentence that my father spoke the night before as he lay next to me in my bed with his hands folded behind his head:

Acceptance of the world is at the heart of our most worthy dreams.

He was like that, my dad. Later on in life I would call him an intellectual—and certainly, of course a poet. But there in the fifties and sixties among the hardworking, vivacious Italians in a poor but happy neighborhood in the northeast corner of Rochester New York he was just "sort of smart," a little quiet and offbeat to some of my belly-minded relatives who worked with him in the shoe factory—but always, "a nice guy." It was not unusual for any of the guys to come around to my house even if I weren't there just to talk to my dad for awhile. I remember coming home one day and finding my dad sitting on the front steps with none other than Johnny Pops himself, just talking quietly, a cigarette between my dad's fingers and Johnny chewing on a long piece of grass. It was a week or so after Johnny's mother died. I suspect they were talking a little about that. My dad was comforting that way. Cosmo always talked to him while I was upstairs changing my clothes. I never heard Cos talk to his own father that way.

So a few minutes later, when Mr. Penfield asked for the papers, I was embarrassed to glance down and read my measly one-page essay; how gracelessly I followed a plagiarized, worldly statement that my father had given me the night before:

> I wish I could float like a 1959 candy-apple red
> Mercury convertible through the streets of bore-
> dom . . .

I had planned to write about starvation, and the sharing of wealth, and the practicality of inter-racial marriage and a single race without prejudice—all those things my dad spoke of the previous night. But all I could think about was riding in Carm's car, the radio up, my arm out the window, a full tank and the sun turning into the moon and the moon becoming the beautiful face of Leona Nassavera.

> . . . I guess an ideal world to me would be one which would be escapable from time to time. Since we're not birds and can't just fly off, maybe we need some way of feeling like we're floating off. I guess most of us feel like that when we drift off into sleep and into dreams that take us anywhere. But to dream isn't enough. The world must be a part of our dreams . . .

I was struggling to relate to my dad's remark. But I hadn't gotten to euthanasia or an end to the death penalty or anything he mentioned and time was running out.

> . . . With our technology Americans can create their own worlds. Pushing a button or stepping on a gas pedal can change everything. Have you ever ridden in a new Mercury convertible? You close your eyes and the streets become clouds. Suddenly you want to peer down at everyone, see everything from a height you never dreamed of reaching, people like ants below you, a single race sharing their crumbs. It's a saintly experience . . .

I rambled on for a couple of minutes more, until I heard Mr. Penfield's voice proclaiming time was up. I finished on a hopeful, generous note:

> I wish there were enough convertibles for everyone, and a summer that would never end!

* * *

The autumn nights are beautiful in upstate New York. The cool, clean air drifts down from Canada and the stars, and we'd send up a smokey, civilized, appreciative signal from a burning pile of Dutch Elm leaves that we had gathered in our thin, damp embraces.

I would have been content to watch the flames dance into the empty hours, sit back on the slight hill in front of Cosmo's house down the street, and half-listen to Johnny Pops singing vulgar lyrics to the songs of Dion and the Belmonts, the smoke filling my nostrils like some incomprehensible perfume. After all, Leona Nassavera sat there across from me on the steps under the moonlight. I watched her graceful refusal of a cigarette as Danny held out, teasingly, a pack he had stolen from his father's desk.

But each moment, we learned early, required its own adventure—as if peacefulness might taunt us with an awareness we could not bear.

Mike, Cosmo's older brother, pulled a small box from his pocket and, as we sat there in our nightly group, so distant it seemed from any worldly concerns, he shook out the .22 caliber cartridges and let them fall to the ground. Johnny Pops, in turn, pulled from his pocket a handful of bullets even larger in size. "This will make it even more interesting," he laughed, letting them fall among the others.

I looked at Cosmo, and looking back at me he let his eyes fall to the ground. We often confided to each other, and he knew the fear I felt toward the game upon which we were to embark. Leona and Barbara Ann abruptly made their way behind the porch, where they could get a good view without any danger. Billy Special (Spezialli, before his dad changed it years back), who was Mike's age, a couple of years or so older than Danny, Cos and me, and the best athlete among us, and though I hated to admit it, Leona's idol as well—Billy gathered up the bullets and tossed them into the fire.

"You first Bright Boy," said Johnny Pops, looking at me and winking at the others. He sensed my fear and this was his way of pushing me. The others, moving behind the trees and out of range, encouraged me further.

"Come on Rosey, don't be chickenshit . . . Let's see a little Apache fire dance, whoo-whoo-whoo . . . " Danny, Billy, Dutch, and Johnny Pops all began chanting with Mike, flapping their hands in front of their mouths like Indians. I glanced over at Leona and Barbara Ann hiding behind the porch and forced a smug smile. It wasn't so hard to appear brave—you just did what you had to do, trusting the gods completely. I had convinced myself, as I was sure Cosmo had, that it wasn't foolishness, it was faith. I began my little dance around the bonfire, a couple of spins and a couple of jumps, trying awkwardly for a little grace, trying to convince myself that Leona was deeply concerned. Johnny Pops called out another endearing *chickenshit*, and I threw a finger everyone's way.

The first one was no more than a snap—and Mike and Danny tried to convince me and the others it had only been a twig crackling, but I knew better and rushed off to the safety of the tree.

Before Dutch circled the fire once, another little explosion went off, and he laughed his red haired, freckle-faced, high-pitched laugh and ran off. Dutch was only a year older than Cos, Danny and me, but he was so big he hung out with the older guys. Being the only non-Italian in the neighborhood, he got teased often—and when he did, he took it out on us smaller guys.

Billy Special was next. He did some incredible back flips around the fire, but in a moment or so, two cartridges went off and it was Mike's turn. Mike, not surprisingly, kept throwing his arm back and forth as if shifting a race car, making roaring sounds as he circled the fire. He was the mechanic among us and had recently bought a beat-up Chevy which he worked on faithfully in his father's garage. "My brother's nuts," whispered Cos, looking on and awaiting his turn.

Mike made so much noise we had to tell him that a bullet went off.

CHAPTER II

As long as you can laugh about it, there'd always been a certain status attached to being a first casualty.

There must have been a dozen explosions or so, and then nothing for a while. Everyone slowly began to gather around the dying bonfire—even Leona and Barbara Ann made their way from the porch. Just as Cosmo, feeling a little confident no doubt, began a fertility dance around the smoking leaves, invoking the names of Marilyn Monroe, Gina Lollabrigida, and Jane Mansfield in a lusty plea for sexual compliance, the last explosion rang out with a crack and a small but distinct puff of smoke. I started to laugh with the others as Cosmo hit the ground like a paratrooper, but when my hand flew instinctively to my burning shoulder, I knew I had been hit.

It was a superficial flesh wound, the bullet grazing my left shoulder. It was Johnny Pops who decided on the Bay & Goodman Grill. "Gentle Jim always has a clean apron around, and there's plenty of whiskey to pour into it," he said, already opening the door of his father's Dodge.

Just about everyone in Rochester agreed that the Bay & Goodman Grill had the best pizza in town. And big Gentle Jim, a roly hulk of a man with blond hair and even blonder eyelids, was the pizza-maker there. From ten in the evening on there was a steady stream of customers both in the restaurant section and where the oak bar loomed in odd elegance amidst the shabby interior of the building. The building itself, a plain, non-descript brick structure built sometime in the early 1900's, was one of those building that seems to last forever—not because of its architecture, which was nothing more or less than a few boards and bricks thrown together in a hasty but precise understanding of communal need, but because it was always a public shelter—laundromat, grocery store, bar—in the midst of hardworking, private dreamers, these Italians with so much energy and so little money. Neighborhoods grew around these structures. Trees surrounded them, protected them from any new fad of structural design. What was basic became the neighborhood aesthetic, like a mailbox on a street corner. Repairs were made matter-of-factly, but with the skill of European craftsmen. Roofs were replaced not with just the elements in mind, but with the thoughts of the things inside that needed protection.

A number of guys gathered around the table to see my wound. Johnny Pops first said *The Monarchs* did it, driving past in a car and taking a couple of shots from the window. They were the archrival gang, and Bambi and Little Christo, two of the older neighborhood toughies, were ready to get together a lynch party, but Danny and Mike were laughing so hard Johnny had to tell them the truth. Gentle Jim came over to me with a clean apron and a shot of whiskey and cleaned the wound, dabbing it with a real medic's touch. When he finished, he held the rest of the whiskey in front of me. "Take care of the germs inside," he said, his pink cheeks glowing, and I took the glass and chugged the whiskey. I must've made quite a face because everyone laughed.

Johnny, Bambi, and Little Christo went over to the bar, and a minute later invited Mike, Dutch and Billy over too. Now Dutch and Billy were only seventeen, and everyone knew it; but at the Bay & Goodman Grill, it was understood that certain rules were under the jurisdiction of the neighborhood. Those were the rules we respected and did not violate. That's why we always left our doors to our houses open on Cummings Street, and the keys in our cars in our driveways. The bartender, Bully, did not hesitate in drawing beers for Dutch and Billy—but he would never have served them had they been by themselves.

"How does it feel?" asked Cosmo, tapping his own shoulder.

"It's okay, okay . . . burns more on the inside," I laughed, "from that rot-gut whiskey. How those guys drink that stuff?"

"You get used to it," said Danny sniffing the shot glass left on the table."

"Who'd want to?"

"Let's get some tripe, this place makes me hungry," said Cos. He was always hungry.

"Gee Rosey, you were almost a statistic tonight." Danny laughed, but kindly, and so did Cosmo. "We coulda had a big goddam gig at Falvo's—got you a casket carved in the shape of Carm's Merc . . . "

"Hey," I shot back, fully relieved now that the wound didn't seem to be serious, "if heaven's like ridin' in Carm's convertible, I'm ready for it man . . . "

"Shit," said Danny, suddenly looking over at the bar, "fucking Billy's chuckin' his beer—I mean shit, look it's gone."

"Even his throat's athletic, goddamn," added Cos, shaking his head.

The waitress came over with three cokes. "From Johnny Pops, boys, drink up."

Johnny Pops lifted a beer in our direction at the bar, "To the wounded in action," he laughed, and we nodded.

"Think your brother Mike will join the Club?" I asked Cosmo.

"He sure is tough enough," added Danny, shaking his head, "he beat the living piss out of Nick Mangione at the playground the other day—I never saw a guy go so crazy. Shit, I think Nick just fainted from lookin' at Mike—probably didn't even see the punches." Danny pantomimed a few punches and kicks; he did it with that infectious laughter of his, and we all began laughing with him.

"But look at him," I said, nodding toward the bar, "you'd never know it—so quiet, such a nice sonofabitch, your brother . . ."

"Yea, but you don't know him when he's angry. Believe me. I forgot to tell ya, yesterday he got so mad at my mom, you know what he did?"

"What?"

"He threw a fucking pitch fork at Old Lady Reilly's cat . . . "

"That old yellow bundle of hair," interrupted Danny, again breaking into a laugh, "looks more like a deformed possum. Hope he got it . . . "

"Na, he missed." Cos gave Danny a stern look. He liked animals. His mother had asthma so he couldn't have a pet. But I'd see him time after time cuddling or feeding some neighborhood mut—including Lady Reilly's cat.

"Well, you gotta be tough to be with the club," said Danny, ignoring Cosmo's glance.

"You gotta be smart too—I mean you gotta have some cool," I added.

"Yea, like Carm."

"Yea, like Carm . . . " Danny agreed. He then pulled his chair up close to the table, bent way forward and whispered, "that's why Johnny Pops never made it in—no smarts, no . . . " He searched for a word.

"No poise . . . no tact." I volunteered in a whisper.

"Yea," repeated Danny, no poise . . . What was it?"

"Tact," I repeated, "no tact."

"Yea, tact . . . " Danny looked at me. "How do you know these words Rosey?"

"I read, you asshole." I said letting a smile slip across my face.

"Well," said Danny, relenting for a moment the competitive spirit between us, "we don't call you Bright Boy for nothin'."

Just then Cosmo looked up alertly toward the end of the bar: "It's your dad, Danny, and he's comin' over . . . "

The Club was the way we identified those who went on from hanging on street corners and the hundred kinds of quixotic delinquency to more legitimate, organized illegal activities, like runnin' numbers, picking up parleys, loan-sharking and other things. In our neighborhood, the Club's headquarters was the *Casa Villione* on Bay Street. There were several such "social" clubs around Rochester. Supposedly they were places for older Italian-Americans to gather and spend the afternoons playing cards. The clubs were also available on weekends for weddings, birthday and graduation parties. But of course everybody knew, including the police, that they housed gambling activities, especially card games and numbers betting. A few months earlier Carm and little Christo got picked up at the *Casa Villione* with fifty grand *in their pockets*! The police would bust the place every once in a while for a couple of reasons: to protect themselves from criticism in a token show of their legal efforts to curb such activities; and to force a hike in payoffs which were made routinely, sometimes from neighbor to neighbor, or even—as some may have suspected the Carlotta boys—from brother to brother. It was rumored that Carm and Little Christo got only forty grand back when the charges were dropped a few hours later.

For the Carlotta family, it was an especially sensitive situation. Both brothers, Carm and Phil, were well-liked, well-respected in the neighborhood. I remember one spring day when a few of us were throwing around a football on the street. Carm stopped by and, since he'd always say how close he'd come to going to Boston College to become a quarterback, he began tossing us a few passes. He was good, a perfect spiral every time. And many of us wondered why he never played at East High School when he was there. But it had been Phil who played for East, a starting halfback in fact. And on this particular spring day, about five minutes after Carm had arrived, Phil too showed up, just out from work and still dressed in his starched and sparkling uniform. Stepping into the street, he took off his policeman's cap and tossed it over to me. Then he trotted a few steps, put his arms over his shoulder, and took a pass from his brother. We all watched as they threw the football to one another. It must have been right after the time Carm and Little Christo got picked up with all that money in their pockets and all the rumors afterward, because as the two handsome athletes tossed the ball back and forth to each other, Phil in his uniform, Carm in his cream-colored jacket and silky black shirt, I began saying a little chant to myself with the rhythm of their passing and catching; it was a phrase I got from looking over a book I found on my father's night table, one too thick to ever imagine reading myself, but the title of which sticking with me, however unconsciously, because there I was repeating it, *crime*, as Carmen threw the ball, *and punishment*, as Phil caught it. *Crime . . . and punishment . . . . Crime . . . . . . and punishment*, until, as the game of catch progressed, the words fell into the arms of each brother, like the ball, without distinction. *Crime . . . and punishment*, I would say, as two brothers flashed their marvelous grins and the words became a kind of poetry in the crisp, clean air between them. *Crime and Punishment*, I sang.

The *Casa Villione* stood at the center of our neighborhood, across from the playground and next to the empty lot. We passed it on our way to the grade school and our way home every day for the first seven years of our schooling. The two-story building was there to catch the balls we managed to hit over the playground fence as we grew older and stronger and less content with our boyhood games. And then we passed the *Casa Villione* everyday on our way to the bus stop during our high school years. And even in the dark we felt the secure, mysterious, chilly brick of its presence as we made our nightly vigil to the *Bay & Goodman Grill*. Once in a while, with somebody's old man, or Carm, we were allowed inside, into the first floor (the hall, which could be rented out, was up-stairs)—and we politely glanced around at the several tables in the large front room where several older men were playing cards and speaking *Italian*. The "real" card games and other entertainments, we understood, were going on in the back rooms. Danny's dad was a frequent visitor to the *Casa Villione*, and I heard Billy's dad say that he liked to test his luck on the horses a little too much. Danny, in fact, said his dad told him there was a little button under one of the tables in the front room where the old men played cards, and if anyone suspicious came in, one of the old men would push it and a red light would start blinking in the back. I imagined that was true.

Carm brought me inside once in a while. He always seemed to go out of his way for me, pay a little more attention to me than the other guys. I certainly wasn't tough or anything, so I was never quite sure why. At the *Casa Villione*, he'd leave me in the front room and go in the back for a few minutes. One time he sat me down with four old men, saying something in *Italian* to them, and whispering to me to see if any of them were dealing from the bot-tom of the deck; then he laughed, brushed his hand over my head and said, "Keep your eyes open now—that's how you learn Bright Boy," and he disappeared into the back room for ten minutes. I did catch one guy dealing from the bottom of the deck, and outside I told Carm.

"Why that old sly sonofabitch, just like him," Carm laughed again in his reassuring way, handing me a dollar bill for, as he said, "keeping a good eye."

It was Carm, as a matter of fact, who gave me the name "Bright Boy." It was at the *Bay & Goodman Grill* one night. I was only fourteen at the time, and Carm was still pretty wild then and still kicked a few asses. He was already making visits to the clubs, and everyone knew he had a future with the mob. We were all finishing up a pizza and someone started arm-wrestling. Billy Special, who was only sixteen but already muscular and athletic, beat everyone at our table, including Johnny Pops. Beating Johnny must have delighted Billy because he pompously challenged Carm. Carm was at the bar talking in a low voice to Godzilla, the robust Puerto Rican bouncer who had a couple of fingers hacked off somewhere a few nights earlier. He turned and put up his hand, as if to say "hold on a minute Billy," but Billy boisterously and a little out of character issued the challenge again.

Carm came over me and sat down and the way he said "Sure Billy" made all of us feel a bit uncomfortable. I don't know, to tell the truth, if Carm could have beaten Billy legitimately that night. They sat there for quite some time with their hands gripped, white-knuckled and red-faced. Their arms strained straight upward, as if coupled in some desperate prayer. Then things happened so quickly it was hard to say why it took place. As they were locked in arm-combat, Carm apparently stomped on Billy's sneakered foot under the table. The flushed young athlete, still with a surprised look on his face, jumped to his feet and took a fierce roundhouse right hook at Carm—which Carm blocked in mid-air, and then lunging across the table, grabbed Billy's head under his left arm and, holding it tightly, twisted his neck and pressed his cheek against the table. Then he did something that surprised us and frightened us for a long time afterward. Carm picked up a beer bottle from another table, busted against the table edge, and held the broken glass against Billy's cheek. Billy's eyes were popping with fear. Nobody in the restaurant or bar said a word. I could see the jagged edge of the glass pressing against the flawless flesh of Billy's cheek.

"You know how easy I could leave my initials across your pretty face forever?" Carm asked, pressing the broken bottle in a little harder. Then he looked at us. "You guys think life is an athletic event," he asked, "like Mr. America here?"

Nobody said anything of course.

"You guys wanna see what the inside of a face looks like? Maybe then you'll remember somethin'—nobody gives a shit how tough you are—cause there's always a weapon around . . . " Then Carm loosened his arm and stood tall and tossed the broken bottle over to Johnny Pops who stepped back and let it fall to the floor. Billy, dazed, sank back into a chair and stared at the floor.

"Use your heads, guys, or you'll die young." Carm said, the quick anger just suddenly gone. "Hey Barb," he called to the waitress, "beers for all these guys, even the young ones . . . Hey Rosey," he yelled over at me with a kind of a laugh, "can you handle it?"

"Yea, sure Carm," I said, trying to sound less shook than I was.

A few minutes later Carm apologized to Billy. Then he came over and sat next to the younger guys. "You know," he said, with a soft, sorrowful voice, a little concerned about the image he presented to us a few minutes earlier, "Billy's a good kid, and a great athlete—everybody knows that, and it's great. But it's got its place, you know—and it won't getcha a bus ride home."

"Shit," he went on, sort of gazing up at the filthy tin ceiling of the B + G, as if it were a sky or something, "if we lived in a fucken forest, I mean with birds singin' to us and fruit hangin' like softballs from trees tall as . . . and rivers, clear . . . " Carm put his hands up as if describing something he couldn't quite see. "I mean," he went on "if we had to swim rivers, and run from bears, and sleep under the fucken stars, then yea, it would be everything, the world a fucken athletic event—and Billy would be king!" He looked at us. "But it ain't. I wish to shit it was, believe me—you know I'm a lot like Billy, I love the physical shit . . . " He took a deep breath. "You guys seen me throw a football—50, 60 yards in the air, right . . . I coulda been startin' at Boston College, no crap. But that's a dream world, this is the real world," and Carm then rolled up his sleeve and displayed a half-foot scar on his left forearm. We had seen it before; he'd gotten it a couple of years earlier in a rumble with the Monarchs. He seemed to hold it before us with a certain pride—as if it were one of his brother Phil's badges.

He looked at us squarely now, finally understanding his outburst towards Billy. "We're just human beings," he continued, "poor decent sonofabitches guys, in the center of a big, ugly city. And we just gotta learn to get by."

Carm put his arm around me. "Look at Rosey here, skinny little shit, huh. Billy'd blow him away with a sneeze, right? Hey I'd take Old Lady Reilly in four . . . "

Everyone laughed, loosening up a little under the wing of Carm we were more used to. I laughed too; each year I got used to the remarks about my thinness—a couple of years back a couple of kids started calling me *Bones*. I hated it.

"But Rosey here," Carm squeezed my shoulder affectionately, "I've been watching him—he looks around, he thinks, he's careful, smart little bugger . . . "

The others coughed and cleared their throats as if to dispute Carm's claims.

"He'll do okay," Carm went on, "a real bright boy . . . "

"Bright Boy . . . ?" Danny spit it out, as if to ridicule the term as it applied to me. But it came out from something deeper than his throat and his voice seemed different when he repeated Carm's term, as if he were half-anointing my new name.

"Yea," Carm said, looking at Danny, "From now on it's Bright Boy—Rosey's a fucken girl's name anyhow . . . You guys want a pizza . . . on me, okay." Carm put his arm up to signal the waitress.

"Sure, great," we answered, still a little bewildered by Carm's changing nature that night. I guess we were hungry enough— everybody was always hungry at the *Bay & Goodman Grill*. I kept hearing Carm's voice saying *Bright Boy* in my head. It certainly was better than *Bones*.

* * *

"Goddam it, what kind of trouble you getting everyone into now Rosey?"

Danny's father looked bleary-eyed at my wounded shoulder as he stood above the B + G Grill. His voice was loud and his words noticeably slurred. He liked to drink as well as gamble.

"Cut it out Dad . . . " Danny started to say, but his father grabbed him by the arm, yanking him to his feet. The chair turned over and everyone looked. Johnny Pops came over to the table.

"I don't want you hanging out with this troublemaker," said Danny's father, twisting his son's arm and staring at me.

"Dad . . . " Danny started to protest, but his father stopped him cold with a powerful slap on the cheek. Danny's eyes blazed back at his father, but he didn't say a word. Cosmo and I had risen to our feet by this time, not knowing what to expect. Johnny Pops grabbed Danny's father by the shoulders and pried Danny's arm loose.

"Don't touch me," bellowed Mr. Polito, too drunk to do much about it, "this is *my* son—and I don't want him hangin' around with that sonofabitch Rosey . . . "

"Take it easy, Mr. Polito . . . everything's gonna be okay" said Johnny, still holding him tightly, struggling with him.

I looked at Danny and he looked at me. We quickly looked away from each other. It happened before. The animosity his father had toward me was a mystery to both of us. He took a disliking to me a couple of years earlier. I never knew why. I guessed he thought I was a wise-guy, and perhaps I did have a few clever comments to offer, but I wasn't the disagreeable sort. I made fun of some sacred institutions—such as the armed forces, President Eisenhower and the federal government in general, the Catholic church, and American Motors cars—but I got that from my father who kept up a family tradition of avoiding a soldier's uniform, openly voting for Stevenson in both elections, being an atheist, and refusing to consider, despite Danny's father's insistence on their quality (he had one of course), buying a Nash Rambler. I know once Danny, in order to avoid punishment himself, said that *I* swiped a pack of *Camels* from their house. The fact is I had asthma and was allergic to cigarette smoke and was the only one of the guys not to puff away behind Cosmo's garage. My dad explained that to Mr. Polito the night he came over demanding an explanation (and a replacement pack of *Camels*)—but, to tell the truth, I think he disliked my dad at least as much as he did me, so he convinced himself that I was a thief, a wise-guy, a "nigger lover," (even before the riots), a communist, and an atheist—or, in his words, a *God-monger*. The blood on my shoulder that night must have confirmed it all.

"Stay away from my son," Danny's dad yelled, so threateningly Johnny Pops grabbed his jacket and pushed him hard against the wall.

"Cut it out—that's enough," Johnny warned him in his angry and boastful way.

Danny didn't know what to do, and if the situation had been any other, I would have gone over to him, put my arm around his shoulder. After all, his dad's dislike for me never affected our relationship—in fact sometimes it bought us closer. But I just watched.

We learned one thing early-on in our neighborhood: to take action no matter how ill-advised, foolish or suicidal, and to avoid being thought of, or worse called, a coward. In the long run, it probably had to do with an integrity essential to the slim thread of manhood most of us managed to hold onto—but in the shorter run such a notion accounted for more lost teeth, broken ribs, swollen fists, and anguish than anyone might have wanted.

So I wasn't surprised to see Danny jump forward and, with tears in his eyes, take a poke at Johnny Pops. Instinctively, Johnny raised his arm to block Danny's half-hearted seemingly (as it struck me later) obligatory punch, and swung his elbow into the pit of Danny's stomach. His father meanwhile, yelled out and swung wildly (drunkenly) as he saw his son double-over and Johnny slammed him back against the wall with more force than before.

I don't know where Carm came from, but just as we stood there perplexed and strangely immobile, there he was, moving to the center of the malady, looming above the three combatants and staring menacingly at Johnny Pops. "That's enough Johnny." He said quietly and firmly, his voice like a distant, peaceful thunder echoing through our own embarrassed silences. Johnny started to say something, but he looked at Carm and walked toward the bar; settling on a stool he mouthed his only protest—"Families—shit. They kill each other." Carm brushed his hand through Danny's hair and looked over at me:

"Take care your friend Bright Boy." He saw my shoulder, but he didn't say anything about it. Then he put his arm around Danny's father's shoulder and walked him over to the bar—far away from Johnny Pops. I saw him raise his hand and order a couple of drinks. He kept his arm around Mr. Polito and talked to him in a low voice.

"Let's get out of here," said Danny, quickly gaining his composure. Cosmo and I got up without saying a word.

"Fucking Johnny," Danny said as we hit the cool autumn night air, the smell of leaves everywhere. "Fucking old man," he muttered. We didn't say anything.

"Fucken Carm too," said Danny.

CHAPTER III

On the last Friday in October we got our report cards and on the way home I did what I'd been doing all the years before: I lied about my marks.

"C's," I said, "all C's."

We were walking home on the first day of the week-long stretch that would end up being the warmest week of autumn ever in Rochester—with the final weekend of it also the hottest of the city's social climate as well.

To tell the truth, nobody enjoyed flashing their report cards around—and I'm sure anyone would have gladly switched cards with me than catch the wrath of a parent's simplistic assessment of a son's educational status. As a matter of fact, a C was a statement that *everything was okay*, and what more could folks from the Bay & Goodman area ask for—the absence of trouble was to live under the hand of God. In the fifties, in a poor neighborhood like ours, dreams were based on fears as much as hopes, so we were careful not to fill our lives with too many of them.

So telling my friends that I had received C's on my report card was not the truth—but it was, as Father Ryan often made the distinction, not a *mortal* sin, just a *venial* one. Actually, I received all A's and B's (with a single C in math) on that warm Friday afternoon in October—pretty much my normal fare.

"Shit," said Danny, glancing down at his yellow card, "my dad'll kick my ass if he sees this. Maybe my sister will sign it again."

"Tell him the F's are for *fun-loving*," said Dutch, flashing his freckled-faced smile.

"Yea," added Cosmo, giving Danny a slap on the shoulder, "and tell him the D's are for *delightful* . . . You are a delightful sonofabitch."

Everyone laughed and Billy did a couple of perfect cartwheels. He always had one A on his card, in gym of course.

"Yea," Cosmo's brother Mike chimed in, "fun-loving, delightful, and F and D, *fucking dumbbell*." I remembered, as we all broke up laughing, how many times Mr. Penfield said we had no feel for language and lacked imaginations. What did he know, I thought.

"At least I don't take four shit-hole periods of auto-shop," Danny snapped back.

Just then Johnny Pops pulled around the corner and over to us in his old man's beat-up Dodge.

"Hey Rosey," he yelled out at me through the window, "Carm's looking for you—he's at the B + G, eatin' tripe." Then he looked at the other guys. "You guys wanna ride home?" he asked, and everyone piled in. At the corner of Bay & Goodman, I got out.

"Hey Rosey," yelled Johnny as they took off, "everybody at the hill tonight at ten o'clock."

"He's probably gotta stay in and do homework," I heard Dutch say sarcastically in that high-pitched, northern European voice of his. I threw a finger as the Dodge turned the corner.

In front of the Bay & Goodman Grill was Carm's red Mercury. I saw my reflection deep and clear in the front fender. When I turned around, there was Carm at the restaurant counter waving me in.

* * *

On the night of the bonfire incident I snuck into bed without anyone noticing the wound on my shoulder.

My dad was sitting at the kitchen table reading a book and drinking coffee—his normal, late-night routine. My sister Judy, who read at least as much as my dad, was lying on the couch in the living room, her eyes so intensely glued to what she was reading I don't think she saw or heard me come in. Usually I'd sit with my dad in the kitchen awhile and have a cup of coffee before I went to bed—a habit I picked up when I was about eight years old. But that night I snuck upstairs and jumped into bed.

Except I couldn't sleep—and I knew why. I wasn't used to concealing anything from my father. It wasn't so much showing him the wound that night. No, that wasn't much different than showing him a spike-wound during baseball season. It was, rather, something else: the fear of coming to a point in my life when I had to keep things to myself. I had sensed for a long time it was coming—the silences at the dinner table a substitute for the adolescent ramblings of our former years. Sure, there were some things that would never surface—like the four Chevy hub-caps I stole to trade for a single Studebaker hub that my dad had lost hitting a bump on Webster Avenue. Or our secret afternoons with Kelly, the girl from the next street who liked to jerk off three or four of us while the others watched.

But this was different. Years later I would see the metaphor as clearly as I could see that night the hallway light in the stairway from my bedroom. I lay there with my shoulder aching along with my conscience. Wounds, however slight, were to be kept to oneself. Like children to be seen and not heard, vulnerabilities were to be acknowledged but not spoken of.

Judy had already gone to bed when I put on my bathrobe and went downstairs to the kitchen. My father was not the type to get overly alarmed, and when I pushed back my t-shirt to show him the shoulder, he merely shook his head as I related the incident.

"Jesus, Rosey," he said, putting two aspirins and a glass of water in front of me, "you know a few inches lower and dumb game or no dumb game you coulda been killed . . . over."

"I know . . . it's dumb." I whispered apologetically.

"But you'll do it again," he replied, in his easy going, strained but calm manner, "you guys are so goddamned bored you'll do something asinine again."

I shrugged my shoulders—my way of agreeing with him—but in doing so a sharp pain shot through the wound and I winced.

"Shit, you okay?" my dad asked, disgusted and concerned. "You know . . . you know it's not that it's dangerous. No, that's not it. I mean God knows we need more adventure in our lives . . . " He folded his hands in front of his face and looked away for a moment.

"I mean my life, Rosey, could have been more interesting—I know that, I do. We get into a rut . . . " He picked up the book, almost unconsciously, and leafed through the pages. I got the feeling, I remember distinctly, that he was struggling not to talk about himself. Years later, when I would experience the recurring dream of dancing around the fire before the penetrating explosion, which always woke me, it was my father who was the most daring, the wildest dancer circling the flames, his laughter an echo of defiance . . .

" . . . but adventure, Rosey, as I understand it, ought to be en-riching—an accomplishment of some sort. Just to prove you're brave by standing in front of an exploding bullet is . . . well, is just an exercise in stupidity. Climb a mountain for Christ's sake, canoe some wild river somewhere—or even stand-up Rosey, you know we've talked about this . . . stand-up, stand-up for something, something you believe in. I mean I'm not telling you not to put something on the line—just don't be stupid about it. Then he touched my shoulder again, looking at the wound with a disgusted but compassionate look on his face.

"What's the sonofabitchin' use," he went on, "you guys will do something as stupid tomorrow—you'll think it's an act of courage in your peanut brains . . . " He got up and lit the coffee water on a burner under a pot on the stove.

"Courage, Rosey," he said, staring at the wall behind the stove, "has to do with ideas, with doing something that makes you more of a human being. You guys do things for a cheap thrill, that's it! Or if it isn't a cheap thrill it's a quick buck. I know what goes on out there . . . "

"What dad?"

"We're killing ourselves out there."

"Where dad, out where?"

"There," he turned to me now and pointed out the dining room window to the street, the dim light of the streetlamp and the night, "out there, on the street—around that bonfire tonight. Look at your shoulder—six goddamn inches from fatality. For what? Why? Cause you're bored, empty! You don't know what to do with yourselves so you do something suicidal in the name of fun, and before you know it you find other ways to kill yourselves."

I had heard my father talk like this before. It was always as if he wanted to say something he couldn't quite get out—something about life . . . about himself. I knew he meant something larger when he said "killing ourselves" rather than simply the physical taking of a life.

"Come here son," he said, holding his arms out. I got up and walked over to him and he embraced me. "I just get frustrated cause I see people throwing their lives away for, for . . . for what?" He seemed surprised by his own question.

"I won't do it again dad." I said, my head nuzzled in his shoulder. I could smell, like always, the sweat under his arm. It always smelled, strangely, like fresh bread.

"It's not just that—I mean tonight was just a boyhood prank, stupid and dangerous . . . I know that. But it's more Rosey. I don't want you to throw your life away for something dumb and momentary—whether it's a display of childish bravery or being tied to a monotonous routine for the sake of a paycheck to fill your house and your garage with trinkets . . . There's something in between."

"What dad?"

"I don't know. I'm not sure."

It was not the first time my father gave me this ambiguous advice: to do something with my life that he couldn't define or articulate. He simply had a feeling that there was a better way.

He kissed me on the forehead. I would never be warm and secure in anyone else's arms, whatever the mystery of his hopes for me. "Rosey, I just want you to look around, see what's going on. And find a way to be happy, not angry, that's all."

"I know dad."

"Here," he said, looking at the small shoulder wound one more time, "use your head Rosey, adventure's one thing, horseplay's another. Maybe this will leave a little scar as a reminder."

"I'm sorry dad."

"It's okay son. You're okay."

* * *

"I saw the way you looked at the Mercury Bright Boy. You want one someday?"

"I wouldn't mind Carm, not at all," I said sitting at a table in the restaurant section of the Bay & Goodman Grill.

"You bet your fucking ass you wouldn't." Carm smiled that confident smile of his.

"Johnny Pops said you wanted to see me."

Carm nodded. "Want a coke . . . a beer?"

"No thanks, Carm."

"Hey Bright Boy, how about making the Sled Run with us this year . . . "

The Sled Run was a tradition in our neighborhood—probably our closest touch with charity, a helping hand. It started with Carm and his brother Phil (before he was a policeman) and Baby Fat Siracusa with help from his dad, Big Red, who was dying of cancer in a penitentiary in Pennsylvania on a charge of racketeering, mail fraud, and a few other things. It began by chance as I understood it when Carm and Baby Fat stole a bunch of granny dolls by mistake from a warehouse. Big Red was so incensed by it (he had sent them for car radios!) that he made them deliver the dolls to an orphanage in the city. It had been a week before Christmas. The nuns, not to mention the kids, were so appreciative of the gesture, once the word got back to Big Red's associates, it was decided that Carm and Baby Fat and a few others would make a visit the following year. I don't know who gave it the name Sled Run, but it became an annual event, and spread to several orphanages and children centers. Of course that meant that the theft grew also. Now, between September and December, several stores and warehouses were looted –mostly with inside connections and small payments (in the spirit of Christmas) to guards, policemen, inventory clerks, etc. . . As a matter of fact, the operation was so successful that some stores volunteered merchandise to save themselves the trouble of broken entries and disconnected alarms. It was a sign of status, not just pride, to be a part of the Sled Run. It stood for something—in our minds at least—unquestionably good. It was not often we were so certain of what something stood for.

So I was bursting with pride that afternoon when I left Bay & Goodman Grill after my meeting with Carm. He dropped me off at the corner gas station.

"Someday you'll be driving one just like this," said Carm as I got out of his convertible, his arm slung across the top of the front seat.

"Thanks Carm."

"Don't mention it Bright Boy."

I ran home clutching my report card like some well-kept secret. My father would appreciate the good marks. But I knew I wouldn't tell him about the Sled Run. He might not understand.

CHAPTER IV

Except for a passing car, almost nothing could disturb our touch football games right after supper under the streetlamp in front of my house.

Usually we'd split up into those who were Cleveland Brown fans and those who rooted for the New York Giants. I was a Browns fan, and I could never understand how Cosmo and his brother Mike and Dutch could argue that Alex Webster was a better full-back than Jim Brown. My father said it was as simple to explain as black and white—Webster being white, and Brown black. In my mind though, I assumed that when the desire was great enough, a person could talk himself into believing anything, and nothing could dissuade him, neither statistics nor direct observation on the Bay & Goodman's T.V. every Sunday afternoon. But when most of us were, afterall, *Calabrese*—that is most of our grandparents or parents came from a part of Italy called Calabria, and they were proud of being known as *hard-headed*, considering it not a term associated with ignorance, but with drive and fortitude, never saying uncle whatever the odds. And, they believed, it built character—the scraped chin, busted-nose kind, every time we pushed ourselves up, like some routine exercise, from the equally routine fall on their faces.

So we played hard and argued lovingly every autumn evening on Cummings Street. It was too, as a bonus strangely enough, an exercise in the democratic nature of God's black-humored ways: Billy Special had bad hands.

He could turn a defensive back in a circle, could block out Dutch with one arm and Mike with the other, and he could outrun everyone once he had the ball.

But Billy couldn't catch the ball for beans. And he couldn't throw a spiral. Time and time again we'd watch the football hit him squarely in the chest, but when he tried to grasp onto it we'd see the ball squiggle through his athletic fingers like a fish. If we'd let him quarterback, his passes would turn end over end in the air, never quite making it to a receiver. And whether that brought him down to our level or us up to his, it sort of evened things up in our minds' scorecards, and so no one ever offered Billy any instruction in these matters. It was nice to know you could cheer yourself up by throwing a pass to Billy and watching him fumble it away.

And if Leona were watching us, I'd throw as many passes to Billy as possible, knowing we'd lose of course, but I'd be scoring my own points.

So that night, feeling good about Carm asking me to be a part of Sled Run, I was hoping Leona and Barbara Ann would show up as we tossed the ball around before choosing teams. Carm came by with Bambi, and his brother Phil, out of uniform, stopped by too. Cosmo's cousin Joey from the west side was visiting and he played too. Before we knew it we had five on a team—Carm quarterbacking the others, who had last pick—and even then had hesitated before saying Billy's name.

No, almost nothing except a passing car could disturb our game. But with our team up by a touchdown, suddenly Phil put the ball under his arm and just stood there, as Dutch paused in the midst of tying his sneaker down on one knee, and Mike and Billy leaned against each other, arms around each other's shoulders—and then we all just stopped and stared for a moment (except for Danny, who picked up a few stones by the curb and tossed them), as we always did, whenever Mary Kay, Danny's beautiful, sexy sister, walked by.

Mary Kay was the neighborhood glamour girl, sex pot, and dream queen all in one—a lovely combination of sex and innocence: Marilyn Monroe and Sandra Dee all in one. She was just eighteen, like my sister Lonnie, in her last year at East High. But she had a worldliness about her that stemmed not only from the fact of her beauty, but from the fact that she dated just about everyone around: from the downtown crew such as Carm and, it had been rumored, even Sammy C himself, to second-class hoods like Baby Fats and Bambi. She even dated Johnny Pops a couple of times. Danny mentioned that very day in fact that Little Christo—chunky, shadow-cheeked, short-haired—had taken her home from school a couple of afternoons that week.

A couple of years earlier she won second place in a city-wide beauty pageant—but since then she had become too sexy to compete with the wholesome competition of pageants. Her long blond hair defied the dark of our neighborhood stares. Her breasts were firm, but heavy, and Danny let us know that there was no stuffing in her bra. Her legs were as shapely as those nylon stockings packages stacked on display shelves in the last row of the A & P, and she usually wore high heels to show them off. She never said too much, but her eyes sparkled so with blue when she looked our way we couldn't seem to say much either. In my mind, etched forever, was the sight of Mary Kay one afternoon when Danny told Cosmo and me to climb up the cherry tree in his backyard; I remember him putting his finger to his lips signaling us to be quiet and then pointing to the bathroom window: there she was, just about to step into the bath, completely naked, one foot on the side of the tub, bent over touching her ankle, her breast perfectly profiled, heavy, the nipple of one, erect, grazing her creamy thigh, and her hair falling onto her golden shoulders. I masturbated five times a day that week, my eyes closed recalling that momentary vision, the slow descent into the bath, the quick darkening of her pubic hair as it touched the water, and the way she cupped one breast and then circled the nipple with her finger. How we didn't fall right out of the tree I'll never know.

Perhaps it was the prize in the beauty pageant that got Danny's father talking about California. But no one could blame him for thinking her beauty was his ticket to Hollywood. I think Danny half-believed it too—at least he mentioned it enough. And when he did, it wasn't like Carm talking about Boston College, or Johnny Pops always mentioning Hawaii. Mary Kay's beauty, her sex appeal, convinced us that a journey to California was not a pipedream.

But even moreso, she meant something more to the rest of us, who out of character, fell into such a hush everytime she passed we didn't even offer a wise-crack, which was our usual response to a silent moment caused by reflection or desire. If she represented simply a fantasy to us, that would be one thing—but here she was, as beautiful a woman as we'd probably see, and she not only walked down our sidewalks, she dated our own kind! Yes, it was her availability that threw us, that made us keep our comments, and our dreams, to ourselves.

We watched Mary Kay's shapely sway and let the clicks of her heels echo through us like some undecipherable clock that measured our time-out—as she disappeared up the steps and into Danny's house. A minute later Phil was backpeddling with the football cocked high behind his head. Johnny Pops was grabbing onto my sweatshirt angrily pushing me out of the way in his lifetime pursuit of his boyhood rival turned cop. And Billy Special ran between Carm and tore upstreet on a fly pattern all alone past the manhole cover and into the end-zone—where, the ball falling with the autumn twilight into his perfectly outstretched arms—he let it tumble right through his hands!

I got up from the street and looked over to make sure Leona had seen the incredible flub. "Nice catch Billy," I yelled, not a bit sorry of course that we failed to score.

* * *

We met that night on the hill, as Johnny asked us to. It was the place we always met.

The "hill" looked oddly out of place—and perhaps it was, as landmarks from another era tend to be. It was a small mound of earth, rising about ten feet from the sidewalk on one side, the corner gas station lot on the other at the corner of our street, Cummings, and Bay Street. On the top of the dirt hill was the remains of a grand Dutch Elm, a tree that apparently had been dead for many years. Its stark, broken limbs and knotted trunk stood firmly, it seemed, at the center of our neighborhood; the oil company enlarged the gas station lot, the city paved over the brick street; Cosmo's uncle Charley built a new house across the street, and one day, at someone's request (we never knew who) some men in Rochester Gas and Electric truck put up a new lightpole right across the sidewalk from the tree, and attached to it a huge streetlamp that threw down an enormous light and equally distinct shadows. I imagine it was done to deter delinquent gatherings on the corner; but I saw it as I would any falling light—as a celebration of the life it illuminated.

But the hill and the tree, I believe—though we never mentioned it—represented a time, a place in our lives that not only would not change, but had not changed. It was a small, secure hideaway in the midst of our bewildering desires to become something we might not be. So it was natural to hang out there when there was nothing to do—a place where we could talk late at night in the sometimes bored, sometimes angry reflection of our youthful exhaustion; a place where we could sing without judgment of the dark cords of our awkward teenage voices; a place we could fight good-naturedly, testing our strength in an endless game of king-of-the-mountain, and a place we could roam to alone, at any time of the day or night, when the world seemed amazingly empty for a while, and one would simply pick at the dead bark and follow the purposeful trail of black ants who seemed to hold onto this hill as resolutely as we did.

Johnny Pops held ten cigarettes in his fist so only the tops of them were showing. As he sat back against the elm on the top of the hill, he held out his hand and one by one, whether we smoked or not, we took a cigarette. I was relieved to see that I'd picked a whole cigarette and stuck it between my lips.

"Sonofabitch," said Cosmo, holding up the broken cigarette, "I knew it would be me."

Billy nudged Leona who was sitting next to him and he laughed and she put her head on his shoulder for a second or two. I turned my head away. Cosmo's brother Mike gave out a hoot and pointed at his brother: "Good, you little shrimp, I hope Johnny's got something good for you."

Barbara had already lit her cigarette and began passing it around to Danny and Dutch to light theirs. Johnny Pops, meanwhile went over to his car parked in the darkened gas station and brought back a cardboard box and a gasoline can. We all looked at each other because Johnny had already made a reputation for himself with a gasoline can and a match the time he burned down the new house being built at the corner of Rocket and Cummings across from Dutch's house. So, for a moment, there was an uneasy silence, and everyone looked at Cosmo because it was a rule that you couldn't back out of the game . . .

We did a lot of things we didn't want to do. We had to be tough—I think I understood it all years later more than I did then. It was a part of our tradition—as immigrants who built lives with hard work, and our American tradition, the rugged individualists. It had to do, I believe, with a healthy cynicism—that no one, no country, no god, would take care of you. It always fell on your shoulders, your strength, your toughness. Unfortunately, the easiest affirmation of toughness was to be cruel and bully others. And we did plenty of that. It was three months earlier in fact, during the summer, when we became less manly in out attempts to be moreso.

Billy, Danny, Cosmo, and I had snuck into a custom auto show at the War Memorial downtown (we knew that place like the back of our hands, and never paid to see car shows, hockey games, or wrestling matches). It was about nine o'clock when we left, still early and a beautiful summer night, so we walked up Main Street toward Clinton Avenue, the center of downtown. We ended up in the lobby of the Seneca Hotel and it was there we first noticed the tall, red-headed kid who, Billy swore, was following us. Danny said something nasty to the kid who was sitting across from us in a corner of the lobby and the way he answered us back we knew he was a fag.

It was Danny's idea to walk the hotel hallways—something we did from time to time to see what trouble, what adventure, we might get into. Hotels, of course represented all the mysteries of strangers, travel, and sex—three things we didn't know much about. We were surprised to see the red-headed kid follow us into the second floor hallway. Danny yelled at him once more and Billy turned and grabbed himself in the crotch in a half-amusing, half-menacing gesture. Still, the kid treated the words and gestures as an invitation and walked towards us. I saw Danny make a fist, but it didn't seem threatening to either him or us and we stood there dumbfounded.

"What do you want faggot?" said Billy as he passed us in the hallway. He was a good half-foot taller than any of us, but pale-skinned with freckles and thin.

"I want to blow you guys," he said, nonchalantly, turning to us halfway down the hall, and then disappearing into a men's room.

"Holy shit," exclaimed Danny, shocked but laughing. "Do you believe that!"

"Let's get out of here," said Cosmo, making his way back toward the stairway. I started following him but Billy spoke up.

"I've gotta see this—come on," and he made his way toward the men's room, and Danny followed, hitting his fist in his hand.

Cos and I looked at each other, shrugged our shoulders and followed our two friends into the men's room. At first I didn't see anyone—just several urinals and two sinks and ourselves in the mirrors over the sinks. But Billy pointed to a stall across from us, and sure enough there were shoes resting on either side of the toilet. Billy pushed the door open and there he was sitting there, waiting.

"Who's first?" he said quietly.

Billy let the door close and turned back to us. "You guys want to get your pipes cleaned?" As he said it he zipped down his fly and pulled out his prick. I was glad to see, thinking of Leona of course, that despite his marvelously built body, his penis was no bigger than mine. I felt relieved, but I wanted to get out of there.

"Watch this," said Billy, and he disappeared into the stall.

We looked at each other. "We ought to beat the shit out of this fag," said Danny.

"You like it?" we heard Billy say in the stall. Then we heard a groan, and we weren't sure from whom it came, but in the next instant we heard two hard slaps and Billy yelled out "You fucken fairy, you like that too . . ."

"Who's next?" said Billy, coming out of the stall, zipping up his fly. Inside we could see the kid holding his head where Billy had whacked him. "But you gotta hit him a couple of times—he likes that better than cock." And then Billy yanked at me and pushed me into the stall.

The door closed and I turned to see the kid sitting there wiping his mouth, which had been bloodied by Billy, with a piece of toilet paper. "Take it out," he said in a whisper, apparently unaffected by the punishment. "I want to see it," and reached out and unzipped my fly. His hands were soft, but quick and expert, and in a second he had my penis in his hand. To my surprise it grew hard immediately as he stroked it.

I clenched my fists, ready to punch him freely, at will, but before I did he put his lips around my stiff penis and I could feel his tongue massaging the underside of the sensitive tip. His mouth was warm and I felt my body reacting, my hips beginning to move—this, I thought, was better than masturbating. And in the next instant, just as I felt myself on the verge of coming, I smashed my right fist into his jaw, and then my left against his head, and pushed him back against the toilet and feeling the anger rise in me like s surge of semen, I kicked him square in the chest and he let out a groan.

"Easy Rosey, leave something for me," said Danny, and I stuffed my penis, still stiff and throbbing, back into my pants before the stall door was pushed open.

"Fucking fag," I said, walking out of the stall, trembling for what seemed a hundred reasons.

"Let me at him," said Danny, brushing past me and entering the stall.

Cosmo too had his turn in the stall that night, and whatever he or the others did or for whatever reasons we never said, and probably never knew. We all beat up the poor sick kid. And for a couple of days we spoke of the incident as if we had virtuously stamped out some disease that night. But I didn't feel good about it, and I don't think the others did either. We had been bullies, and we didn't get any tougher by that experience. It struck me that we learned a little that night, about the world and ourselves: that there were some sick people roaming the streets of downtown Rochester; that there just wasn't enough sex in some people's lives and that it didn't take much to take advantage of someone pathetic and helpless—and we would not feel very good about doing so.

. . . Poor Cosmo's mouth dropped open. We all looked at each other, and I waited for someone to speak up, to call the whole game off. But nobody said anything.

Johnny Pops pulled the cat from the cardboard box. Dutch said what we all had recognized:

"Hey, that's old lady Reilly's cat, right?"

"Sure is," replied Johnny, "the one that tips over every garbage can on the block at least once a week. Ugly little creature, isn't he?"

Nobody said anything. We looked at Cosmo who was just staring at the cat. It was no secret about Cosmo's feelings for animals, and everyone had seen Cos with old lady Reilly's cat in his lap at least once.

"What we gonna do?" gulped Cosmo, looking at Johnny.

"Don't worry Cos, nothing much—just scare the little monster a little, that's all"

"Look at my brother, what a chickenshit," said Mike, kneeling next to Johnny. "What's the gasoline for Johnny?"

"Maybe we shouldn't . . . " Leona blurted out, but Billy cut her off:

"Hey, this is guy stuff, stay out of it, Cosmo's not a kid."

And to my disappointment she did exactly what Billy told her to do.

"We just put a little gasoline on its tail like this," said Johnny, pouring a little from the can on the furry tail, "and Cosmo lights it with this match and we'll see one fucken scared cat . . . "

Cosmo sat there, looking down at the ground now. Even in the shadows I could tell he was pale. But I knew too that none of us would back out of that little game of dare that we played.

"Let me do it Johnny," I said, moving over to take the match, "I never liked the cat . . . "

Johnny pushed me back hard and I somersaulted backwards. "Fuck off Rosey, you know the rules." And then he gave the matchbook to Cosmo.

"What's the matter—not quite man enough Cos? Your brother would have lit it already."

"Fucking eh," Mike nodded.

"Leave him alone," sulked Danny.

The cat looked terrified, hunched tensely under the hand of Johnny Pops.

"Don't do it Cos," I said glancing at Johnny who was glaring back at me.

"Shut your fucking mouth Rosey," Johnny yelled, "Cosmo's not a baby-ass chicken like you, right Cos . . . "

"Go ahead Cos," implored Dutch with his horsey laugh, "just scare the fucken critter, that's all."

"Come on sissy," taunted Cosmo's brother, and then Mike reached over toward the cat with his lit cigarette, "Shit let me show you how . . . "

Cosmo grabbed his brother's arm and knocked the cigarette out of his hand. Then quicker than Mike or anyone else could react, he put the cigarette to the pack of matches and when they burst into fire tossed them at the cat's tail which lit up into flames immediately. We jumped out of the way as the cat made a mad dash down the hill, his tail on fire. The cat ran frantically in a circle in the gas station lot and before anyone could say anything keeled over and just lay there while the flames began to flicker.

"My God, did you see that . . . " uttered Danny.

"Holy Fuck," said Mike—even he was amazed at the cat's burst of pure fright.

Both Leona and Barbara Ann turned away. Billy walked over to the cat as the flames on its tail went out and poked the animal with his finger. "Deader than a goddamn doornail," he said.

"Your garbage is safe," beamed Johnny Pops, trying to get a laugh—but everyone was shaken by the experience. We looked at Cosmo—and that was more frightening than the cat on fire.

He had a strange grin on his face—and his head was kind of nodding up and down slowly, as if he were understanding something. Danny went over to him.

"You okay Cos?"

Cosmo pushed Danny's arm away, and the grin never left his face as he spoke: "Shit yea . . . hey, it's only a cat . . . did you see that fucker run in circles. Jesus wasn't that something . . . " And he kept nodding his head like a blind man.

Nobody said anything. I looked at Johnny Pops.

"You're a fucking asshole Johnny." I said.

He kicked me hard in the stomach. When I got to my feet, doubled-over, I fought back the tears that were welling, like two ancient oceans, behind my eyes.

CHAPTER V

I knew I shouldn't have done it. I couldn't imagine anyone would take it as anything but a friendly gesture—but of course it was more than that.

"Sure Rosey, I'll go to the Goodie Shoppe with you—I love Mexican frappes."

Leona was my age, sixteen, and the prettiest girl I knew. She had short, light brown, almost reddish hair. And her face was delicate, sweet—with a small straight nose that defied the neighborhood. Her mother was French—something special, a nationality mysterious and classy, and never ridiculed in our neighborhood like Poles, Irish, or Dutchmen, like Dutch. She and Billy, I hated to admit but had to, made a handsome couple. But I had come to the conclusion a long time before that they had different temperaments, and were not really suited for each other. I knew it wouldn't do any good to tell her that. I had to impress her.

"Don't say anything Leona—I mean I gotta keep this kinda quiet you understand—but Carm wants me to be a part of Sled Run."

"Really Rosey—gee, that's nice."

Old Mr. Briscoe, the proprietor of the Goodie Shoppe, brought over our Mexican frappes—vanilla ice cream with chocolate sauce covered with Spanish peanuts and whipped cream.

"Yea," I continued, trying not to stare at her blue eyes that made everything else unimportant, "it gives Christmas a special meaning, you know. I mean all those poor kids with no gifts or nothin' . . . "

"Is it dangerous Rosey?" she asked, licking some whipped cream from the corner of her lovely mouth.

"Naw . . . we're just careful, quiet . . . quick. It's not that scary when you're doin something good—you understand."

"I'd be afraid Rosey. To be truthful, I don't like a lot of things you guys do in the neighborhood. The other night for example, that's the worst thing I ever saw, setting that cat on fire like that.

Johnny shouldn't have done that to Cosmo. I'm glad you spoke up Rosey, that was brave of you. How's your stomach?"

"Oh, it's okay." Suddenly I felt a warm glow in my cheeks—*brave, brave of me.*

"Rosey."

"Yes Leona?"

"I've been meaning to ask something—kind of personal . . . "

"You can ask me anything Leona. I mean we're friends, aren't we?"

"Yea Rosey, sure." She looked at me. Her hand was less than an inch from mine. I wanted to put my hand over hers, and bend her across the table and put my lips on her cheeks, her lips, her French nose.

"Rosey . . . it's your name—I mean I wish you had another name for me to call you, cause 'Rosey' . . . well, Rosey sounds to me like a girl's name."

"I'll change it . . . " I blurted out without any composure whatsoever. "I mean I've got other names—some of the guys, you know, call me *Bright Boy . . .* "

"Come on Rosey, that's not a real name . . . I mean a real, ordinary name. Like Nick, or Frank, or Richard, or Billy . . . "

"Leona, those *are* ordinary names—I like something different."

"Like Rosey?"

"Well, maybe not *Rosey* . . . "

"What's your real name Rosey? Your real name can't be Rosey."

"It's . . . it's *Rosario.* After my grandfather. He looked just like Clark Gable," I added.

"*Rosario,*" she repeated, to my surprise, with disgust—"that's worse than Rosey. Anyway, you don't look like Clark Gable Rosey."

"Is there another name for you?"

"Yes."

"There is?"

"Yes."

"Well Rosey, what is it?"

I hesitated. It was a name I disliked so much I embraced the name of Rosey as an alternative years before. "It's *Ross*," I whispered.

"What?"

"Ross . . . you know R O S S—my parents said it's short for Rosario, but it always sounded dumb to me."

"*Ross . . . Ross . . .* " she repeated, saying it to herself, then to the air, then to me: "Ross, *hi Ross . . . hello Ross.* Thank you for the Mexican frappe *Ross . . .* "

"Yea," I said, embarrassed. "not too . . . "

"*Ross*, it's a great name Rosey, a nice short, strong name—sounds like another country, Europe even. I like it Rosey, I'm going to call you *Ross.*"

On our way out of the ice cream parlor we passed a couple of friends, and I took my time saying hello to them with Leona by my side. I was hoping everybody in the world would pass us on our way home just to see her walking next to me—just the two of us. I was already thinking of how it would be to borrow Carm's Mercury some day and just drive her around when outside the door Billy met us. And he was angry!

"Sneakin' around Rosey? I heard you were here with Leona. Behind my back, huh runt." With his powerful arm he pushed me against the front of the building.

"Billy," interrupted Leona, "we was just talkin', that's all, honest—Ross, uh Rosey bought me some ice cream . . . "

Billy grabbed me hard by the collar. "Next time you want to buy Leona some ice cream, or anything else, ask me—you got that?" And he shoved me to the ground in front of the Goodie Shoppe.

"Leave him alone." Leona protested, but Billy grabbed her hand abruptly and pulled her down the sidewalk on what was to be *our* walk home.

I sat there for a moment, thinking of how Carm warned Billy, and us too, how it wasn't enough to be physically tough. But I knew that if I had said something, Billy would have beat my ass right there in front of Leona.

And that would have been even worse.

* * *

"Come in here son, I want to show you something."

I followed my mother into her bedroom. She did not spend much time talking to my sisters and me. She seemed to leave that to my father. She saw herself, I think, as someone who maintained not simply a house, but an environment where all basic needs were taken care of so that other activities, the dialogue, the humor, the care, could go on unencumbered. When her kind diminished from the earth, I convinced myself later on in life, everything would be chaotic, only practical matters would receive a kind of frantic attention, and our lives would be impoverished.

She reached up into the closet and pulled an old shoebox.

I sat on my parents' bed, on my father's side, next to the nightstand, upon which stood a statue of Joseph holding the child Jesus. Why an atheist would have such a statue next to his bed I didn't know—but I did ask. My father's answer was always simple—"Because he believes in fatherhood."

"I'll show you something Rosey . . . "

"*Ross*, mom call me Ross."

"Oh Rosey . . . Ross," she said, putting her hand on the back of my head and rustling my hair, "you'll always be my little Rosey."

She took out of the shoebox a couple of notebooks, dusty and obviously quite old. She held them against her chest.

"I want you to see these, but don't tell your dad I showed them to you. He may show them to you or your sisters someday but that's up to him. I'm showing them to you Rosey because I'm beginning to see how much like your dad you are."

"What are they mom?"

She opened one of the notebooks, looked at me, and smiled, warm, caring like always, but almost mysteriously. "Listen Rosey, tell me what you think." And then she read with a voice I had never heard from her before, or from anyone. She spoke each word with a care she gave to dusting her bone china, and I knew for the first time that language rose from the heart and escaped the body, touching the lips and then the air through a breath of pride and accomplishment. It was so utterly human. It was the first poetry—despite all those English courses—that I had ever experienced.

"Home," she said a little uncomfortably, and then she looked at me with a pause that follows a title.

I didn't know what to expect—words about the house I was sitting in, about my sisters and me laughing at the kitchen table, about my mother's staunch countenance being the silent background against which the rest of us read our books late at night. I was surprised, even upon hearing that first piece of secret writing by my father, at the steady, isolated, lonely voice as my mother spoke the words of my father:

> On a long empty table
> I place my elbows,
> two stakes bearing claim to my place
> on this wood swept clean
> by the steady winds that blow,
> always, toward the past . . .
>
> On the wall
> the darkened continent of my shadow
> remains unexplored.
> I map my journey around it,
> and there I am:
> sitting at a table, alone,
> in the new world.

My mother obviously read them before. Her voice flowed more gracefully as she read. It was, I observed from that day on, the lyric that filled her, not the message. She, true to character, read from the heart, not the mind. "Here's one, Rosey, I think he wrote when you were a baby, about holding you in his arms. Listen . . . it's lovely," she commented, looking at the old notebook as if it were a family relic.

> . . . he doesn't hear the words
> I slip between his ear

and the hundred white birds
flying across his eyes,
but lifts his chin and stares
beyond me
and I turn for a moment:
my shadow has risen
like an angel in a dark robe
and flown off.
I hold you now, son,
in the adequate light
of my own two arms.

"Dad wrote those?" I burst out, just to hear myself respond. "They're . . . I mean I think they're . . . uh . . . nice—beautiful even!"

"They are Rosey," replied my mother, handing me the old notebook. "your dad had, *has*, a real gift."

I looked through the pages. There must have been a hundred poems written down. I read a few lines at random, aloud, but not really to anyone, except that inner self so remote and understanding. The titles, unlike the scribbling of the poetry itself, were beautifully printed—as if belabored with a final, formal touch.

"Did he ever show these to anyone?" I asked, struck by the fluid images of phrase after phrase as I turned through the pages. "I mean, did he ever publish them or anything?" "No," my mother laughed in her gentle, reflective manner. "He sent them to magazines, but no one took any. Your dad said they were more like Italian poems he had read as a youngster, and he thought his poems were not like those he could find here and there in magazines and libraries—and eventually he stopped sending them anywhere, and then he stopped writing as well. He had no one to show them to besides—you know your uncles Rosey. He read them to me—but my praise, well, he knew and I knew, was for him more than for what he wrote. I just didn't have anything very smart to say except they were beautiful."

They were. Almost unconsciously I found myself reading another one, its title, *Ignorance*, like the others beautifully printed:

A small fire leaves the shape of its last flame
upon the distant glacier
receding through my eyes.
Through the darkness of my ribs
an old season moves clumsily.

From my hand a leaf falls,
a glove of my former colors;
it quivers on a stone of ice.
I am neither warm nor cold.
My blood flows for an answer.

I too was filled with that strange pleasure, that pleasurable *igno-rance*, of coming across something beautiful that I did not understand. It did not matter, the incomprehension—I could see the obvious care, the sincerity that went into the making of these poems, a care that almost certainly did not go into the shoes my father made at the factory. I think, in fact, that he hated his job, though he never complained. And though I was sure of his love for all of us, now I wondered even more how he felt toward his life, toward whatever it was that moved him to write so. My blood, like his, would flow for an answer.

"Don't tell him, Rosey," said my mother, "it's very private thing for him—sometimes I think he'd like to forget them for some reason. They'll be up here—you can look at them when you want to, but let him show them to you someday. I think he will Rosey."

"Look at this one," she said, taking the notebook from my hand and turning to a page she knew, it's for me, though your dad has never admitted it. Here," she said, wiping her eye, pride's tear, "you read it Rosey."

I read through the first few lines. It was a love poem, that was for sure. It was even more lovely than the others. I couldn't help but begin to recite the rest of it aloud as my mother stood there. Afterall, it was her poem:

. . . my eyelids, cloth of dreams, wear thin,
until you become the clearness of my sight.
You still come forward; from where?

Each touch leaves my hands and forms
the shape you enter before me.
The moon goes down,
our eyes open.
If the wind were to speak
it would ask your name.
I would answer you have none;
you are the one
from which the others, in the blindness
of love, acquire faith.
And the wind would add:
then worship her in my name.

I gave the notebook back to my mom. "That's really something mom—who woulda known . . ."

From that afternoon on I would look from time to time at the notebook filled with poems hidden in the closet of my parents' room. It was a father's voice that I have never imagined—but the more I read, the more it sounded like him. From that day on, his voice, even in the most casual moments, like sitting around the table after supper, his voice took on a new resonance, as if it had been released from a dark, thoughtful breath deep within a man we would never thoroughly know. The next time I looked at the note-book –which was the following afternoon, I memorized one short poem I came across. I guess because it was one I could understand, even then in my adolescent perspective of the world. It was titled— that elegant printing at the top of the page above the scribbled lyr-ic—

Destination

The next step comes,
and with it comes
another journey.
I turn away from it,
endlessly. This is no journey.
I am dancing.

* * *

Johnny Pops apologized to me for kicking me in the stomach a couple of nights earlier on the hill. Whether he meant it or whether he just said it because he needed a favor, I don't know. He wasn't a bad guy—it's just that he wanted so much to be the one we looked up to in the neighborhood. The trouble was that we were getting a little too old for some of his street pranks, which had entertained us for many years previously. I knew already that I didn't want to be like Johnny—who was about the same age as Carm give a year or so. But he had nothing to show for it.

"Go get Danny, I need him too," said Johnny, seemingly in a hurry.

"I can't," I answered, "his dad's home—he doesn't want me near the house."

"Shit, his old man sure carries a grudge—strange guy. What you ever do to make Danny's dad so angry with you?"

"Nothin' Johnny. Except be Danny's friend. I did accidently bloody his nose with a baseball once—but that was years ago when we were kids . . . I don't know, honest."

"Okay I'll get Danny. Be back in a minute. Put on a clean shirt, okay?" It was another one of Johnny's "insurance" schemes— which we must have learned from his dad who was an insurance agent. Johnny brought us over to the shopping center and parked across from the *A& P*.

"Here," he said, giving us fifty cents, "you guys gotta be doin' somethin' legit - so go inside and get a couple of candy bars. But don't eat 'em until I tell you to."

The plan was simple. We were to sit on the curb eating candy bars, *perfect witnesses*. Johnny would wait for the right car pulling out of the parking area and jump in front of it, bounce off, and roll to the ground feigning injury. "Don't worry, I've done it before," he said. A couple of cars passed him slowly, but he seemed to be waiting for a certain kind of driver. When we saw the old woman stretching her head over the steering wheel and pulling out of her parking space across from Johnny who was waiting in his car, we thought that might be the one.

When he jumped in front of her and banged off her front fender, he let out a shriek as he rolled to the ground and several people rushed over, as we did, anxiously, not knowing whether Johnny was really hurt or not. He lay there moaning, half curled up holding his ribs, and some older black man bent over him to see how badly he was hurt. The old woman, who stopped immediately, got out of the car and with the help of a cane limped over to where Johnny lay. She said a few things in Italian, but the black man stooped over Johnny just turned to her and shrugged his shoulders, obviously not understanding a word she was saying. At first I thought his incomprehension angered her, because it soon became obvious that she wasn't very concerned about Johnny who was moaning at her feet. She started gesturing wildly, first toward her car, then toward Johnny. A few English words began sprinkling through her hollering—*stupido, monkey, jerko,* and so forth. Not an ounce of sympathy for her victim—just wrath. I saw the look on Johnny's face begin to change. He hadn't expected this.

Nor did he expect to be hit with a cane, which she soon began doing with vigor, swearing in Italian at the same time. The few people who had gathered were startled—one moment looking terribly concerned, the next breaking into an uncomfortable laugh. Johnny, with an absolute look of amazement on his face, held up his arms to protect himself. The woman was shouting now, totally enraged. It was then we heard the siren and saw the ambulance turn from Goodman Street into the shopping center.

Johnny jumped up, motioned to us, and started running. No longer witnesses but accomplishes, we started running too, behind him and certainly not as fast. Back at the gas-station, we found him drinking a coke and relaying the story to Jack the station owner and Bambi and Little Christo, who were cracking up. Jack was searching through the junk drawer beneath the cash register for a band-aid for Johnny's arm—a small cut, his only injury: from the old lady's cane.

* * *

"Everybody knows about it, I know—but not a word anyhow, you understand . . . Not where we go, who we visit, nothin'. Got it?"

"Yea Carm," I said sliding onto the leather seats of the Mercury.

"I don't say a word, not to anyone."

It was the warmest, sunniest autumn ever in Rochester, and hardly a day passed without the convertible top on the Merc being folded down and tucked under the white cover that bore the initials *C.C.* I could see myself behind the wheel. I could imagine Carm holding out his keys and saying "Be careful Bright Boy," and me with my arm hung over the door gliding down Cummings Street and slowing down in front of Leona's house, and her sitting on the steps, returning my wave with a sigh that rose harmoniously with the soft echo of the glasspack mufflers . . .

"I want to see what it's like—the good and the bad of it. Nothin's easy," Carm said, turning effortlessly the leather-covered steering wheel as we headed downtown.

At the warehouse, on a back street where I could see the Genesee River tumbling over the falls under the bridge over the Main Street, we pulled up to a delivery stall. "Stay here," said Carm as he walked over to a steel entrance door and pushed a buzzer. Somebody in a blue uniform, probably a security guard of sorts, appeared almost immediately and greeted Carm with a subdued but friendly handshake. They talked for a second, all the while the guy in uniform nodding his head. Then Carm pulled a wad of bills from his pocket and handed a couple of bills from his pocket to the man, who quickly stuffed them into his own pocket. They shook hands again, and by the time Carm got back to the car, the man disappeared back into the warehouse.

"Lesson number one, Bright Boy," said Carm as he slipped behind the wheel, "keep it friendly and profitable."

I must have looked a little befuddled because Carm looked at me and laughed and went on to explain: "Rosey, uh . . . I mean Bright Boy, right . . . "

"Bright Boy, no one wants any trouble, you understand—everybody's alike as far as that goes . . . Wanna ice cream?" Carm interjected, pulling into the *Carvel* parking lot.

A moment later, licking the double chocolate cone Carm bought me (he insisted on a double), I sat tall as I could in the front seat of the Merc and he continued.

"People have good hearts, Rosey—if I didn't believe that I'd be doin some shit, kickin' ass just to feel better, ya understand?"

I nodded, but I didn't really understand.

" . . . and when things aren't quite right, aren't quite fair, people, down deep I mean Rosey—people want to make things fair. And things ain't fair unless everybody comes away with a little something. As long as it's just a little something, nobody feels bad. Take a little, give a little—and nobody gets hurt."

"So in our Sled Run, we just don't take, we give a little too, on the front end I mean. You see me slip a few bucks to that watchman?"

I nodded.

"He gets a little and he's happy. He leaves the door open one night, closes his eyes—we get a few boxes of stuff and everybody's happy—especially the orphans on Christmas Day—not with some banged-up, repainted junky toys the cops and the firemen collect, but with *brand new*, in the box toys—first class, I mean *first class* Bright Boy, like those kids deserve on Christmas, those poor little shits . . . "

It seemed to make sense to me.

"The trouble is Rosey, uh, Bright Boy, is that people get greedy —they want more than they deserve. Then there's trouble. And everybody's greedy these days. Shit, it's a national pastime, like baseball—and that's why we remind people that if you make it, you gotta share it, simple as that. When people stop sharing, they get hurt. It's in the bible Bright Boy, a lesson as old as the fucken bible itself."

I could see, sitting there that beautiful fall day with the top down and the sun shining and the ice cream melting on my tongue like some glorious, unspeakable affirmation of life, that there was a serious, philosophical side to the dude Danny referred to as Cool Carm. It was just that he never could explain himself very clearly. But it was, I kept telling myself, the heart that mattered. And at the core of the annual Sled Run, I knew, was the heart of Jesus, America, and Carm Carlotta. This would be the best Christmas ever—I could feel it. Under the big blue upstate sky, the mellow roar of the glasspack mufflers turning the heads of the girls waiting in line at the ice cream counter, Carm lit a cigarette as we pulled away and the smoke drifted off behind us like an incredibly fine white silk scarf . . . And I could feel it.

* * *

From the first day I snuck a look at my father's poetry I wanted to mention it to him. But I didn't. Several times I made my way to the closet—always when he was at the shoe factory of course—and I read a few poems; each time the magic of the language seemed a little less strange, each time the voice of my father and the voice on the page coming closer together, like glass lenses in a camera, until one distinct image appeared to the viewer.

And he didn't mention it either. Even when he helped me with writing assignments and I asked how something might be stated *poetically*. He simply laughed, brushed his hand through my hair and said, as if to dismiss the notion completely, "So, you want to be a poet, huh, Rosey." And then he'd laugh.

But he did confess something: And by doing so cleared up a mystery that had always bothered both me and my friend Danny for a long time.

"Now don't say anything," my dad said as we sat with a cup of coffee at the kitchen table at midnight, "especially to Danny now . . ."

I had been expressing my bewilderment at being banned from Danny's house by his father, and brought up, again, that awful night at the *Bay & Goodman Grill* when Dan's drunken old man caused such a scene with me cast in the villain's role.

" . . . but years ago Rosey," my dad continued, "when we were kids, even though we were from different neighborhoods—well," he corrected himself, "maybe *because* we were from different neighborhoods, we had a fight, Danny's dad and myself. Not a street fight mind you, but a real boxing match—in the old garage behind the delicatessen on Bay Street. A referee and everything."

"Really dad?"

"Yea," he laughed, "his friends on one side, mine on the other."

"What happened? You win?"

"I broke his nose—first round," my dad chuckled.

"No . . . you're kiddin' me dad."

"Honest Rosey, the fight must've lasted a minute or less—then wham, I threw a right and his nose was a bloody mess. That was it. A few of his bigger friends threatened me after that, but my friends where there too, so everybody went home, his dad's nose wrapped in ice."

"Wow," I said, startled both by my mild mannered father's fisticuffs and the explanation of Danny's father's wrath toward me.

"You know," the thought hit me, "his nose is a little crooked."

"I really caught him one," my dad chuckled again, like a kid.

"It was a short fight Rosey, but apparently the grudge has lasted a long time."

"No wonder . . . " I echoed my dad's assessment.

"But let's keep it to ourselves, huh son—it would only embarrass Danny. And if his father found out we told Danny, he'd probably come over here and shoot us."

"Okay dad, it's our secret—but that sure does explain things."

"Well, Rosey, don't expect such simple explanations," my father cautioned me, "there'll be a lot of mysteries you'll have to live with, especially when it comes to people's feelings."

And as he said that, one mystery crossed my mind—one I kept to myself, like the one-round knockout, like the shoe-factory, nothing to show for his thoughtfulness but small, strong, calloused

hands that he placed on my shoulders as he kissed me on the forehead and said goodnight.

* * *

I carried the crowbar over to the back door, but as soon as we
reached the door, the big guy, the older balding guy Carm introduced to me as "Curley," took it and pried open the door with ease.
Bambi, tattoos evident on both dark thin arms, went first with the
flashlight.

"Come on, don't worry," Carm whispered to me in reassuring
voice, and I followed him in.

It was a large discount store at the end of Goodman Street
heading toward the lake. I had been there with my family several
times, but never after midnight entering through the storage ramp
in the dark. I could feel my teeth and knees shaking as if they were
attached by a single nerve that continued up through the part of
my brain that controlled the imagination. I kept thinking about
those orphan kids and the spirit of Christmas, and stayed as close as
I could to Carm.

"Everything's cool," said Bambi, coming back from a wall
where he shone the flashlight against what might have been a burglar alarm system, "nobody knows we're here, you-know-who took
care of the wiring."

"This is it," said the muscular Curley, sliding four big boxes
over towards us. "A piece of cake," he added, picking up one of
them.

"Get inside the back of the van, Bright Boy," Carm said to me,
"help get 'em in there."

I situated the boxes as best as I could as Bambi and Curley lifted them into the back of the van. The whole thing must've taken
five minutes. Someone, obviously, had arranged the boxes and disconnected the alarm—probably some unhappy shipping clerk, I
thought, who was glad to stash a few of Carm's bucks into his
pocket.

We left Bambi and Curley on the corner of Portland and Clifford, the same place we picked them up. Carm dropped me off at the gas station and slipped me a five dollar bill. "Get to bed, Bright Boy, you got school tomorrow."

Although it was late, after midnight, I sat on my front steps for a minute under the bright three-quarter moon and the insignificant glow of the streetlamp. It was still unreasonably warm, as if summer had never ended. A couple of minutes later, to my surprise, I saw Cosmo walking all alone across the street.

"Cos . . . that you?" I yelled quietly, the way one does late at night in his own neighborhood. He stopped and we met each other under the streetlamp. He had a bag under his arm, and he looked a little uncomfortable, as if he were trying to hide something.

"What you doin' buddy," I started to say, but Cosmo put his finger in front of his lips to keep me quiet.

"Listen Rosey, I was gonna let you in on this, and ask ya ta help me out as a matter fact—but I wasn't quite ready yet," he said nervously, looking over his shoulders, "give me another few days, huh . . ."

"What the hell you talkin' about Cos?"

"Well . . ." There was sweat forming on his temples. He didn't seem to know what to say.

"Okay Rosey . . . You gotta keep this secret—between us, just us, okay . . . promise?"

"Sure Cos, you know I will. What's up?"

"Look here." He took the bag from under his arm and opened it under the streetlamp and close to my face. When I looked I almost choked. I guess I let out a little shriek, and Cos muffled it with his hands over my mouth. In the bag were a couple of dead rats.

"My god," I said regaining some composure, "What the fuck is this Cos?...rats? Dead rats? What's goin' on?"

"I got them behind the station—you know, in the junk pile where they throw the old oil.. I think these suckers live on that stuff . . ."

"I don't care where you found them Cos. Why? Why do you have them in the bag for Christ's sake?"

"It's . . . it's . . . " Cosmo seemed in a nervous daze of some sort, as if grasping for an explanation that he just couldn't utter. Suddenly I heard my name, the sound filling the street and Cosmo quickly shoving the bag under his arm as we stood under the light of streetlamp. It was my father, calling from the front steps of our porch.

"Rosey, it's late, tomorrow's a schoolday, come on in . . . is that you Cos?"

"Yes . . . Hello Mr. Tarcone, "Cos yelled back. Then he turned to me and whispered, I'll explain tomorrow—don't worry, it's okay, you'll see." Then he looked right at me for the first time that night: "I want you to help me out Rosey—you'll see, I'll tell ya tomorrow." And then he disappeared quickly down the street.

"What are you up to tonight Rosey, out so late and all?" my father asked, once we were inside the house. What was I to say? That earlier I helped to burglarize a discount store—in the spirit of Christmas of course? And just then I was inquiring about the dead rats Cos was carrying around in a paper bag!

Secrets. Early on we begin to live with them. First as convenience, later to ease the embarrassment, the guilt, the fear. Secrets that begin in the quick of the eyes, that slip into the deep involuntary breath of the speechless, that fill the heart with hope and clutter the mind with implausible plots. My father, I was sure, unlike Danny's old man, was as understanding a man as any. Still:

"Nothin' dad, just hangin' out," I answered.

CHAPTER V

Every fall in upstate New York the trees catch fire—the flame spreading south from the Adirondacks until a thousand shades of orange, red and yellow fill the countryside with a spectacular reminder of time and change. The pumpkins ripen and swell in the discarded, weed-filled corner of the garden; the apples weigh down their ancient branches, the bushel barrels stacked casually alongside the edge of the orchards; and the scent of grapes, too sweet, heavy with their own outdated bulk, rise with the mist of the finger-lake valleys and drift in that intoxicating southerly breeze toward the alluring light of the city just north.

But this October, in Rochester, the flames were real. Not bonfires on the corners of the neighborhood streets or matches lit discreetly and the slow burn of tobacco in the dark of Cosmo's garage, but flames rising from Palermo's Grocery on Central Park and Portland Avenue—from the storage bins of the Public Market—smoke rising from Tony's Gun Shop on Bay Street after the initial explosions, and flames shooting up through the siren-filled night from the rectory next to St. Francis church.

There had been sparks in the summer. The *Monarchs*, our neighborhood gang, of which Carm had been a member, and of which Johnny Pops, Bambi and some of the older guys were still, had twice confronted groups of blacks—shooting and wounding two of them in a bloody gang-fight just a few blocks from Bay and Goodman, which was acknowledged as one of the borders of *our* neighborhood. That was in August, just two months earlier, and most of us assumed that the cooler air of September would prevail.

But October was like any other August that year, and the restlessness of the neighborhoods began again, gangs of youths, mostly black, roaming the streets of Rochester, starting fires, looting stores on occasion, and even turning over two police cars. It was the last weekend in October when it all exploded, right after a sixteen year-old black burglar suspect was killed by an anxious policeman. Being next in line as far as the hierarchy of the poor, our neighborhood of course adjoined the black neighborhoods, and subsequently our anger, our frustrations, blossomed in a similar manner, and our hostilities, naturally, as the system requires, were directed toward them.

I remember my disappointment on that Friday night the curfew was imposed. Our family had planned an overnight trip to Corning to see the glass museum and the fall foliage (what little there was that year). My mother, though, who became quite nervous at the slightest notion of trouble, cancelled the trip immediately, seeing instead to the locks on our doors and windows—even to the laughter and teasing of the rest of us, especially my father. But his good humor was not to be found anywhere else on Cummings Street, nor anywhere in the neighborhood in fact.

By Friday afternoon, the porches on our streets looked like arsenals. Cos, Danny and I walked down Bay Street to the Bay & Goodman Grill early that evening, and we counted a dozen houses where people were sitting on their porches with guns in their hands and laps. Mr. Benedetto, Bambi's father, who owned the bowling alley on Culver Road, called us over from his porch steps. He was cleaning a rifle, a police-band radio blaring on the railing behind him.

"You boys be careful now—up there," he said pointing up Bay Street toward the black neighborhood—"ain't no place to be tonight—those 'tutsoonies' are restless sons of bitches . . . listen to those wardrums."

Tutsoonies was the Italian term, derogatory of course, for blacks.

The "wardrums" were sirens, police cars and fire trucks, and could be heard sporadically for the past 24 hours throughout the city.

"Those sirens you mean?" I asked.

"Sirens, ha, ha, wardrums . . . call 'em what you want son—but the natives are restless, and the war is on." Mr. Benedetto grabbed his rifle, placed it on his lap, and padded it with his heavy, shapeless hand—the way one might touch a pet. "I wish those jungle-bunnies would show up in my front yard—I'd give 'em something to shout about, he said, staring up Bay Street as if expecting to see a stampede of natives pouring out of the jungle.

"Look at this," he said, excitedly now, like a kid with an audience of kids. He opened an old fishing box that was next to him on a porch step. He pulled out what looked like an iron baseball.

"Here Danny, catch." He tossed it to Danny, who was standing between me and Cos, a few feet away from the sitting Mr. Benedetto.

"Wow," said Danny, catching it and weighing it in his hand, "it sure is heavy—what is it?"

"I think I know," said Cosmo, his eyes a little wider than usual.

"Me too." I added.

"A vintage, genuine, World War two high intensity, shrapnel hand grenade," said Mr. Benedetto, beaming.

"Holy shit," said Danny, looking at the grenade in his hand.

"Don't worry, the pin's in it—it's okay." Mr. Benedetto assured Danny, who slowly and gingerly, handed the grenade back to him. "How'd ya like ta toss this in the middle of some rampaging tutsoonies!" he laughed as he curled his arm back like Bob Feller. Then he looked at us. "be careful now fellas . . . "

"There's a sick sonofabitch," I whispered to my friends as we left Bambi's father's yard and made our way to the Bay and Goodman Grill.

"Jesus," Danny said, "do you believe he actually tossed me a hand-grenade!"

"Glad we weren't niggers," exclaimed Cosmo, "he woulda tossed it alright—with the fuckin' pin in his teeth."

We passed a few more porches. It was like a holiday— neighbors gathering in each other's yards, sipping beer (one guy cooking hamburgers with a couple of bats leaning against the grill), gesturing the way only Italians can. But instead of pushing back a leaf to inspect a ripe tomato in a small, impeccable backyard garden, or men burying their heads under the hood of somebody's Chevrolet, this time everyone was checking out their rifles. Mr. Santangelo's porch looked like a weapons depot. He waved to us as we passed: "Any problems boys, you come see me." And then he resumed loading a gun.

When a car backfired, we all jumped. Then we looked at each other and laughed. It wasn't that we were frightened. It was the paradox of our existence: any kind of action, of experience, was better than nothing, better than routine. But it seemed like the only action we could initiate had to do with violent, aggressive confrontations. And here it was, in our laps. In the name of law, of liberty (at least in our minds) we could kick somebody else's ass for a change. We could relive our frustration on one hand, and fill ourselves with pride on the other. I could see it in the faces of Mr. Benedetto and Mr. Santangelo—it wasn't just their yards they didn't want violated, it was their beliefs, however far removed from their actual lives, that a system was working that insured success and justice for those who worked hard and kept to themselves. It was the old way, tried and trusted, as ancient and real as their stately, sun-burned foreheads and classic Roman noses. The rioting blacks were ridiculing that notion, and these working class Italians would have none of it.

" . . . you guys are too young, go on home," said Johnny Pops. He turned back to Mike, Dutch and Billy, who were not only old enough, but apparently in on something. From the bar Bambi and Little Christo motioned to Johnny while they drank beer and downed a couple of shots. They seemed restless, ready to go.

"Where you goin'?" Cosmo asked his brother Mike.

"We're gonna patrol the area—cruise a couple a cars, make sure they keep in their own territory. Let 'em burn their own fucken houses down."

Then I saw something that had never happened in the Bay & Goodman Grill before. Johnny Pops took a pistol and loaded it right on the table, in front of everyone. Nobody said anything, but I could see the anxiety of our older buddies—Mike, Dutch, and Billy—who were being initiated into something more grand than the stealing of hub-caps.

"Tell him not to do it," I whispered to Cos, who gave me a funny look, as if I had said something he did not understand.

"Tell Mike," I repeated myself, "not to go—it's trouble and it's stupid," I said, finding myself repeating the words of my father as he had spoken them a couple hours earlier.

"Stupid?" said Cos, in a voice that made the others look over. "What's your suggestion—we give those niggers a welcoming party?"

I looked around. Everyone was staring at me. I wished I hadn't said anything. I felt like stuffing Cosmo's mouth with napkins.

"What's Bright Boy doing," asked Billy in a sarcastic voice, "taking sides with the natives?"

"I'm not takin' sides with nobody," I yelled back, not wanting any aggravation, especially from Billy. "All I'm sayin' is you can butcher every nigger from here to Portland Avenue and nothin's gonna get better for you Mr. America."

"At least I stand up for what's mine, you wimp." Billy stood up now, and glared over me.

"What are you Rosey," asked Mike, pointing his finger at me, "a nigger-lover?"

"Nigger-lover," laughed Dutch in his high, nasal laugh, "Rosey's a nigger-lover..."

"Leave him alone," said Danny, coming to my defense, "that's not what he means." Cosmo just looked at me. He didn't say anything.

"Say what you want assholes, all I'm sayin's that you shouldn't throw your lives away because of them. They're just distraught, depressed," I said again repeating my father's words, "we're just repressed." I looked around—it was obvious no one understood a word I was saying. But I kept trying: "If we were desperate, we'd be breaking windows too!"

"Why don't you admit you're just afraid Rosey," said Billy, menacingly. He was still upset apparently about my ice cream date with Leona.

"I'm not afraid of any tutsoonies," I yelled back at him, standing up, "and I'm not afraid of you and your muscle-bound pea-sized brain . . . "

He made a rush for me and I put up my fists instinctively. But fortunately for me Johnny Pops stepped in front of Billy. I noticed too that Danny stood up as well, protectively. I felt relieved when Johnny sat Billy down at the table. He looked at both of us disgustedly. "There's a hundred niggers out there waitin' to smash in your skulls and you guys are squarin' off. Come on," said Johnny, placing his pistol back in his holster, "grow up you dimwits. Billy save your anger for out there, for them," and he nodded toward Bay Street. "And Rosey, Mr. Smart-Ass," he said, pointing his finger at me, "keep your bright thoughts to yourself—or share them with your bookworm sisters, or your old man, or whoever the fuck thinks the way you do. But we gotta neighborhood to protect here, and if you're gonna take sides with goddamn niggers, then go over there and fight with 'em."

By that time everybody in the place was looking at me—and not with any sympathetic expressions either. I didn't say anything, and a couple of minutes later the older guys went off with Johnny, Bambi and Little Christo to patrol the streets.

* * *

Later that night, in Cosmo's garage, Danny uncorked a bottle of wine he stole from his house. Leona and Barbara were there with us, and we passed the bottle back and forth between the front and back seats of Cosmo's father's old green DeSoto sedan. I sat in the back with the girls, my arm casually atop the seat, Leona's hair brushing my hand with every laugh, each sip from the bottle.

We could hear the sirens going on sporadically through the night, and several times Cosmo grabbed the steering wheel of his father's car, as if, instead of sitting inside that dark garage, he were cruising down Bay Street himself, looking for intruders like his brother Mike, Dutch, and Billy. "We oughta be out there," he kept saying.

"What do you think *Ross* . . . " Leona began to say, but of course Danny and Cosmo weren't going to let that pass.

"*Ross*," said Danny breaking into a grin, "*Ross?*" he repeated mockingly, "what do you think Ross?"

"*Ross?* Is that you *Rosey?*" added Cosmo, "Or is she talkin' to someone else?"

"Why don't you guys cut the crap," said Leona, in either her defense or mine, what's wrong with the name *Ross*—it's better than *Rosey*—that's a girl's name . . . "

That brought forth another fit of laughter from my two friends in the front seat, and Barbara too. The wine was having its effect. I took a long chug and passed the bottle to Leona.

"Why not call him *Bright Boy*" suggested the laughing Danny.

" . . . or *Bones*," burst out Cosmo, and that started everyone laughing, including to my chagrin, Leona!

"Fuck all of you." I said, taking the bottle back from Leona and guzzling down more wine. The laughing fit, enhanced by the wine, must have lasted five minutes. And when Leona couldn't stop herself from giggling, and put her arms around me in an attempt to apologize (which she couldn't do without bursting into another giggle), I joined them, taking the opportunity to hug Leona back, and even brush my lips against her hair—without her realizing anything, I assured myself.

In a few minutes the humor subsided, and suddenly we were sitting there staring straight ahead (stoned, the following generation would say)—not at the darkness of the dank garage, but at whatever it is a person sees when silence forms its easy lump in your throat, and the overstuffed car cushions take you deep into their insular comfort, and there is really nothing to see except that strange horizon, hazy distinction between darkness and light, between what you know and what you desire. All of us sat there looking straight ahead into the void of the windshield of Cosmo's father's DeSoto. It was well after midnight and the sirens could still be heard intermittently against the stillness of our lives. The wine eased its way through our young blood, and added to our exhaustion, if not bewilderment. I don't think any of us were thinking any more of the black-faced strangers clutching rocks in their mighty fists. It would not be anger, I knew even then, that would sustain us—anymore than it would sustain our unsuspecting dark brothers. There we were, five teenagers too young to cruise and protect the riotous streets of our city, too old to ignore the smaller riots brewing in the overcrowded dwelling of adolescence. We sat there, our friendship a comfort as we drifted away from each other, following in that black windshield whatever roads we could create in our raw imaginations. Even Leona seemed to disappear for a moment. I don't know how far we travelled, on what journeys upon which each of us was stumbling, when Danny said, as if a voice in a dream . . .

"See the mountains . . . "

No one said anything. His words were an interruption—not so much a surprise as an adjustment of our visions.

"Sure," I said, breaking the silence, "I see 'em."

"The Rockies," Danny said, staring straight ahead into the darkness, "the Rocky Mountains," he went on, "you can see the snowtops, the glaciers, those jagged peaks poking the clouds . . . "

"We're comin' up on 'em," said Cosmo, picking up on Danny's imagination, perhaps seeing them himself as he put both hands on the steering wheel and guided us.

"I've never seen them before," said Barbara, sitting forward and looking over Danny's shoulder, "I've never been outa New York State."

"Me neither," added Leona, "I've never seen the Rockies." She moved a little closer to me, her shoulder against mine. But, like the others, I stared at the darkness of the windshield.

"They're huge," I said, reaching forward and touching the shoulder of Cosmo, who was driving with care now, with ease. "I've never seen such mountains—there's no way to get over them."

"You've never seen me drive," said Cosmo, "I can take you anywhere . . . "

"Not there," said Danny, and everyone listened, because they were *his* mountains, it was *his* journey.

"Why not?" asked Barbara, disbelievingly, "Tonight we can go anywhere."

"Not there," repeated Danny, suddenly pointing at nothing.

"Look closely, way up on the tip—the roads are all ice . . . glaciers . . . and the snow, look at the drifts at the end of each highway. Where are we going . . . "

"To the other side, I'm drivin' . . . you watch me. All the way to the other fuckin' side, to California . . . "

"That's just it Cos . . . "

"What?" I said.

"Yea, why not Danny?" added Leona.

"There's nothing there . . . "

"Nothing there?" Leona's voice was calm, searching; she looked at Danny now instead of the darkness we were staring into. "What about the west coast—the western divide. California? What about Hollywood Danny—isn't that where you and Mary Kay and your Dad's going?"

Suddenly what seemed like a playful fantasy loomed darkly in our deep-rooted concern for each other. If *Hollywood* did not exist for Danny—then what in God's name could possibly exist for the rest of us?

"It's not there," Danny spoke in a soft, serious voice, "beautiful peaks, that's it—nothing but a drop-off on the other side, one big, dark fucking ocean."

"No California Danny?' My voice seemed as strange as his, more gentle than I'd ever remembered hearing it. "What about Mary Kay . . . "

"Come on Rosey," Danny said, turning to me, a melancholy smirk across his face, his hand falling on my arm, "California's a pipe dream for us—Hollywood," he went on, a sincere, genuine chuckle in his voice, "Hollywood doesn't even exist."

No one knew what to say. All that talk about going to California, and in one mood-given moment sitting in the dark in Cosmo's garage, the truth seemed unbearable. Cosmo tried to change spirits—"You know what I see . . . "

But after a few minutes of our own lost indulgences in the vast dream-tinted windshield, we got out, opened the garage doors and headed home, the wine and our exhaustion finally overcoming us.

I walked Leona home. We both mentioned Danny, and said how badly we felt about him feeling so sad. But we were thinking of ourselves as well. That's why we were surprised by the kiss we gave each other. It came suddenly, from both of us, in front of her house next to the streetlamp. I remember the strange speechlessness of it all, her lips softer than anything I had ever touched, the buzz of the streetlamp overhead, and in the background, one last siren to remind me this was not California, or Heaven for that matter, but the northeast side of Rochester, New York.

I'm sure we were both surprised by such a simple expression of passion on a night reeling with a range of emotions. We certainly did not know that the last siren, sounding so distant into the night that surrounded us with the anonymity of our own unrealized fears . . . that that siren would affect us so deeply.

* * *

When I looked up, it was my father above me, and for a moment I thought it was the recurring dream of being lost again . . . But he was waking me, tugging gently at my shoulders.

"Come on Rosey—downstairs. Danny and Cos are here. Some bad news son. Come on . . . "

It had been a pleasant rest that night—reliving Leona's kiss over and over, covering my own arm with kisses in a series of intensified dramatic replays. I must have lain awake quite a while. Like most young romantics, I assumed one kiss would warm the heart forever. I had been waiting for such a long time. I must have thought of a dozen excuses to go to her house the next day. The thought also occurred to me that Leona, after drinking the wine in Cosmo's garage, had been too drunk to remember the kiss, and I would have to wait once more—perhaps another two years!—for another opportunity.

But that fear quickly passed in the notion that some important part of my identity had been revealed to Leona—the warm, caring, passionate part of me which, for all of us, had such a tough time rising to the surface. Indeed, wasn't that the reason, considering the repression of those qualities in the name of manhood, that men (or boys really) crumbled into marriage on their first romantic (and sexual) encounters. I thought of my own identity—*identities* really—represented, it had occurred to me as I lay restless in my bed, by the different nicknames I seemed to be picking up in my early life. *Bones*, the one I hated—because of its graphic description which was, I knew, a little more accurate than I cared to acknowledge. Dutch gave it to me—that pale skinned, freckled, red-haired northern European with the flabby flesh. The trouble was, it caught on, and I suffered through a couple of years of hearing it—not just in the neighborhood, but at the playground and even at the school. I confided in Cos and Danny, and it seemed when they stopped using it, so did others.

And of course there was *Rosey*—my real name—from my first years in this world because, according to my mother, I had such rosey cheeks, and, being the boy my parents had always wanted, I was the "prize rose of the family." More than that, it was the sound, *Rosey*, that carried with it the love and concern I heard in the voices that surrounded me. I knew it was a girl's name—but it didn't bother me to think of changing it until Leona objected to it. But although I would turn responsibly forever at the sound of it, I wanted to be called something else.

But *Ross*! So short, and blunt. Rhyming in a way with *sauce, boss, moss, loss* and even *horse*—which I discovered, when I looked up in my mother's 'names for baby' book, it actually meant in its Scottish origins (the skirts, the bag-pipes, ugh!), and I certainly didn't see my skinny self as a horse—nor did I want to.

But then it was Leona's choice. And afterall, didn't she see a part of me that others didn't. I felt I should respect her taste, even if it meant putting up with the ridicule that I encountered when others heard her say it, *Ross*, the previous night in Cosmo's garage. Maybe, my romantic mind suggested to me, she simply wanted to have her own name for me—something different or new. Something *continental* I convinced myself, hearing myself whisper *Ross* and I gave my arm another passionate kiss as I lay there contemplating the future with Leona.

To tell the truth, the name I liked, the identity that pleased me, was the one Carm Carlotta coined: *Bright Boy*. Despite my lying about my grades every report card period, I was sure there was a certain power if not prestige in being quicker in thought than those around me. Carm's name for me was the first acknowledgement of the validity of that notion. It was, I thought, a congenial recognition of a strength I possessed—in fact, the anti-thesis of *Bones*. That's why however sarcastic any of the guys mimicked the name *Bright Boy*, nobody disputed it. I recognized, of course, my father's intelligence. But I saw it had only caused him frustration and disappointment in his own life—the solitary neighbor, a strange relative, no one to sustain or argue his insightful quirks into human nature. His most beautiful pronouncements of his life, his poetry, locked up in some dusty shoebox in the dank closet of a mortgaged home. No, I would not allow myself to suffocate in whatever intelligence god granted me. I would turn it into something. My god, I told myself, this is America, land of ideas and ingenuity. If Carm wanted *brawn*, he would have chosen Billy, or Mike, or any of the others for Sled Run. But he chose *brain*—and I would show him he made the right choice.

. . . Coming downstairs to the kitchen that Saturday morning I found Cos and Danny sitting at the table with my sisters, all looking glum, and my mother, dabbing her eyes with a kleenex. I could see that Cos had been crying too. My father held out a cup of coffee for me in one hand, and the newspaper in the other.

Before I could finish reading the heading headline—RIOTS ESCALATE: TWO YOUTHS KILLED—Cos blurted out what everyone in the room knew except me: "Billy's dead Rosey—last night, right in the chest . . . he's dead."

I sat down, glancing at the first page and seeing, sure enough, Billy's photo—right next to a photo of the black youth, who was killed also.

"He got it last night," said Danny, stoic but shaken, "sometime after midnight—didn't have a gun or nothin'. Just walked up to a couple of niggers up by the playground to see what they was up to—and *bang*, one of 'em took out a gun and shot 'em– once— right in that big chest of his."

"Who shot him?" I asked, pointing to the photograph of the other kid killed, "this kid?" "No . . . " said my dad and Cos at the same time. No one said anything else. My mother was crying softly to herself. My sister Judy got up from her chair, shaking her head disgustedly. "Stupid fucking kids—you too Rosey!" she said, walking out of the kitchen. My mother began to protest Judy's language, and I saw Danny's and Cosmo's jaws drop—but my father just put out his hand as if to motion to let her go, and nobody said anything.

"How did this guy die?" I asked, pointing again to the black youth. For a moment, everyone just sat there. Then Danny spoke up:

"One of us—nobody knows who, or nobody's sayin'. After Billy got shot, somebody shot that kid for revenge," he said.

"Jesus," I said, feeling suddenly faint, "Jesus Christ, poor Billy."

"Of all the guys to get shot," added Cosmo.

"It's always somebody," said my father in his metaphysical manner.

"It coulda been us," said Danny, getting up and walking over to the stove to pour himself more coffee.

"We weren't out there last night," I added, trying for a degree of realism at a moment when nothing seemed real.

"Well, it coulda been," Danny shot back, then adding "Goddamn, poor Billy."

For the neighborhood, the loss of Billy would be felt for a long time, but the significance of his death along with that of the black boy (Kingston Brown, 18 years old, a year older than Billy) would not affect us the way it would the rest of Rochester. That night, Billy and the other youth's photos filled the television screens as well. Mayor Lang eulogized the youths and announced that bronze statues of the youths would be constructed on either side of the Liberty Pole in the heart of Rochester on Main Street. It would be a reminder for all of us, he went on to say, of the tragic consequences for the young when social and racial unrest rises to violent levels. No one benefits, he said, when neighbors do battle, and from this day on (he spoke on Saturday night, the day after the killings) the status of Billy Special and Kingston Brown would symbolize the absurd price uncivilized behavior would demand of us—along with the pride we must take in our city to make sure our youth would not waste their lives needlessly. It was a stunning, emotional speech—surely Mayor Lang's best, people remarked.

And it must have been because the riots subsided almost immediately. Saturday night there were a few scattered fires and looting, and by Sunday the curfew was lifted. On Monday morning the Mayor arranged a funeral ceremony at St. Joseph's on Clinton Avenue in downtown Rochester—for both Billy and the black kid. Several thousand people showed up—black and white together, and despite the elaborate security measures and mighty show of police, there wasn't a hint of violence or, for that matter, bad feelings.

As a matter of fact, several times during the sermon and eulogies, a number of blacks and whites held hands, embraced each other, and cried together. And in one ingenious gesture, the city had arranged for pall bearers from a white gang (The Monarchs) and a black gang (Satan's Disciples) to carry the caskets of both dead youths in and out of the church. That's the scene the national television networks picked up on, and we watched it on both the 6:30 and the 11:00 news, looking for ourselves in the background. Carm's brother Phil worked hard to convince the Monarchs to participate, and apparently a black cop convinced Satan's Disciples. Ironically—although this was something we kept to ourselves—Fast Eddie was one of the pall-bearers for Kingston Brown, and rumor was that he pulled the trigger. The other possibility was that it was Mike, Cosmo's brother and Billy's best friend. Like the others, I didn't want to know. And it seemed no one wanted to know either as the investigation into it and Billy's death seemed to wane as quickly as the riots quelled.

* * *

The huge line of cars following one another with their lights on split at Dewey and Ridge roads, the whites heading toward Lake Avenue and the older, shady sections of St. Sepulchre's Cemetery and the blacks staying on Dewey heading toward the newer section with the small flat stones amidst the absence of trees. Even in death, it occurred to me sitting between Danny and Cosmo in the back seat of Johnny Pops' Dodge, there was a separation of the races—except in death the blacks went to the suburbs and its newly cleared space, and the whites returned to the older grounds and the shade and solitude of the beautiful, sprawling (however diseased) elms.

The morning of Billy's funeral I got up early—not just to get ready and have my sister Lonnie make a Windsor knot in my tie, as she always did when I had to dress up for something, but especially to talk to my father before he went to work.

Naturally, Billy's death had an effect on all of us. But as much as we could commiserate with each other, at sixteen death was something you took inside of yourself to try and fathom. The sense of immortality begins to fade at puberty, and by the time a young person's voice changes, the silence around that voice begins to deepen also.

I did not think for a moment, as the priest at St. Phillips, the neighbors, and especially my friends' mothers had stated, that God had called on Billy to join him in heaven for good cause. I felt, like Mayor Lang I guess, that, simply, a life—two lives that is—had been wasted. It didn't make any sense, and that's what bothered me: the fact that something senseless would affect us more profoundly than any sensible realization we might spend our lives working our asses off to attain. "It isn't death which is meaningful to us," my dad told me the morning after Billy was killed, "it's its alternative." I remember waiting for an explanation, but he didn't

offer any. Sometimes I'd get angry with him for his seemingly infi-
nite wisdom and his limited ability to articulate it all. And this had
been one of those times. We were so deeply touched by the loss of a
playmate—and I wanted someone to give focus to, or arrange, or
provide an insight into the swirling emotions I felt inside. So on
the morning of the wake, when I knew I'd hear one piece of bull-
shit after another from priests and politicians and a few neighbors
too dumb to correctly memorize a cliché, I wanted my father to
utter a few goddamn intelligent words which might illuminate the
meaning of Billy's death.

"Nothing," he said, sipping his coffee.

"What do you mean 'nothing'," I exploded, my sisters and my
mother suddenly staring at me. "You sit there calmly," I went on,
determined to get him to say more, " and I know you know something—but you sit there as if I'm asking you the ball scores."

"Rosey, my god you've got promise!" interjected my sarcastic
sister Judy, "maybe you *will* graduate at the middle of your class
. . . "

"Shut up four eyes." I stared at my father.

My mother walked over and put her hands on my shoulders.
"Take it easy Rosey, we know you feel bad . . . "

"I always feel bad," I exploded once more, this time jumping to
my feet and freeing myself from my mother's limp grasp, "especially when I know there's more to something, and there's more to
this, I know it . . . "

That's just it Rosey," said my father, also getting up and walking over to me, grabbing my shoulder firmly but gently until I
faced him. "There's nothing to make of it, life and death are acci-
dents—take your sister for instance," he said, pointing at Lonnie
who was looking back surprisingly at him, "she was an accident, a
wonderful, delightful one," he smiled at the old family joke, "but
an accident."

"Sam!" my mother cried out, suddenly red in the face.

My father looked at me, his expression changing. "Do you
think this is school, Rosey, some lesson we can all write down and
memorize and repeat verbatim the next time? A lesson? What? That

we shouldn't go out when it's dark? That we shouldn't, or should, carry a gun with us? That God acts in strange ways? Come on Rosey, those aren't lessons, they're fears."

"Well, what is there then?" asked Lonnie in her sincere, poised manner.

"Very little honey, as far as I know. Billy was a boy blessed with strength, and grace, and physical abilities none of us ever possessed, and it's a shame we won't see him do a backflip on the sidewalk in front of the house, no matter how he loved to show off. That was the treat he offered us in life. But his death is, well, just meaningless. We can cry and grieve over his loss—but it won't enlighten us. For the moment there's a little peace between our neighborhoods, but that's more fright than wisdom."

"You'll never be mayor dad," said Judy, wittingly.

"That's for sure," my mother tried to laugh.

"I guess, Rosey," my father looked at me, his voice lower now, his sincerity on his sleeve, "if I tried to understand it—" he paused, and seemed to wince, as if the words were painful, difficult to find. " . . . it's taking the good and the bad together, knowing they don't exist separately. If it's a perfect backflip like Billy's that pleases us one moment, then its absence makes us feel hollow—without it, we wouldn't miss it. One doesn't exist without the other. That's life."

"A true existentialist, I should have known," said Judy, picking up her books as a horn sounded in front of the house.

" . . . so we feel bad," my father went on, oblivious to Judy's remark even as she kissed him on the cheek as she made her way through the kitchen, "because something made us feel good in the first place. It's not that we shouldn't grieve over our losses—if I know you Rosey your eyes won't be very dry at the cemetery today. It's just that one person's death—even mine or yours Rosey, won't make us much smarter. The statues of Billy and that black kid are the mayor's downpayment on the governorship more than anything else, son. Our image of Billy doing a backflip is much more meaningful." He put his arms around me and I hugged back. Lonnie left for school and kissed me on the forehead on the way out.

My mother went upstairs, and my father filled both our cups with coffee.

"I'm glad, Rosey," my father said, his voice taking on a confidential tone now that we were alone, "that you're giving thought to these things. I've felt for a long time that being curious is more important than understanding—which will always seem to elude us afterall."

"You make me curious," I said. My father laughed, as if he were laughing at himself, a figure to be curious about.

"No, really." I insisted

"I'm not surprised," he laughed again. But then he asked "what do you mean?"

"Nobody around here thinks the way you do. At Cos' house conversation is a rehash of the morning sports page. Dutch's old man spends his time reciting household chores. And Danny's . . . well, that's another story." From my pocket I took a piece of paper I had folded carefully that morning, and I placed it on the table next to my father's cup. He just looked at it.

"What is it?" he asked, finally.

"It's a poem Dad."

"A poem?" He picked it up, the paper still folded, but he made no attempt to open it or read it.

"Something you wrote Rosey?"

"Not exactly dad—I copied it over," I replied.

"Can I look at it?"

"Sure, go ahead—that's why I'm showing it to you."

He read it. He did not look up at me after he recognized that it was his poem, which I'm sure was immediately. Instead, he read on slowly, his lips moving to the sound of the words as he spoke them to himself. He must have looked at the poem for a couple of minutes before looking up at me. When he did, that warm smile of his appeared.

"Good poem, huh?" he laughed.

"Sure is," I said feeling a strange sense of relief but not knowing why. I hadn't known what to expect—what does a man do when he's exposed as a *poet*? Deny it? Confess? Claim it was an accident?

"So you found them huh? Wrote that one for an uncle of mine when he died—though, to tell the truth, I never knew him much, or thought much of him in fact."

I nodded my head, adding. "Mom showed them to me—said not to say anything until you showed them to me. They're good dad . . . I mean terrific . . . "

"I spent some time with them son—more time, more care than anyone knows, including your mom."

"Why did you stop?" I asked.

"Oh, I don't know. Got tired of the privacy mostly. No one would publish them—no one would even look at them really. No big reason, no big deal."

"Well, they seem special to me dad—I've read through them all, several times."

My father laughed his quiet, tender laugh, and leaned forward and ran his hand through my hair, "Good . . . then I wrote them for one good goddamn reason, didn't I," he joked.

"I'm gonna read this one at the gravesite today, dad—I think it's appropriate. Is it okay?"

"I never ever read a poem in public . . . "

"I won't dad, just say the word," I quickly offered.

"No.. no," he said, leaning back and sipping his coffee, and then shaking his head. "No son—nobody ever asked me, that's all," he laughed to himself. "No ... you go ahead, read it if you want. I'm flattered, really."

Then he looked at me and winked. "But do me one favor son—don't mention that I wrote it."

"Well dad . . . sure, if you say so," I folded the poem and put it in my pocket. "But who should I say wrote it dad?"

"You,' he shot back with that wise, warm manner of his. "Let them think you wrote it Rosey, what the hell."

* * *

" . . . at least *here* there's some respect for the color of a man's skin," I heard one of Billy's uncles whisper as we made our way to the gravesite. People formed a circle around the freshly dug grave; next to it, the mahogany casket glistened—once again, Mr. Falvo, the undertaker, must have successfully equated expense with love; Billy' family was poorer than most in the neighborhood, but with burials and funerals, it never seemed to matter much. Kingston Brown, I had noticed, had a similar casket.

At the center of the circle, directly across from the head of the casket, and right next to Billy's mom and dad and little brother, was Leona. She seemed lost in the blackness of her dress and long gloves, the dark stockings and the veil that came down across her lovely face. At the wake, I couldn't bring myself to say anything to her. I don't know if she had given much thought to the timing of our first kiss and Billy's death (which, I agonized over, must have occurred within minutes of each other)—perhaps the grief and accompanying pageantry of Italian condolences took her mind away from that matter; but I knew that sometime sooner or later I would appear in her dreamy melodrama of guilt—not a role, of course, I would have chosen for myself.

As the priest began eulogizing Billy for the last time, I couldn't help think of the significance of the cold wind suddenly blowing in from the lake and the dark clouds rising from the horizon. I watched a rush of leaves twirl in a colorful dance into the open grave. Behind me I heard Cosmo sniffing, trying to keep the tears away. There was a small symphony of moans and cries until Billy's mother cried out his name and, like a strange dark applause, the whole crowd seemed to groan together. It was then the priest and Mr. Falvo, who'd arranged it for me, looked over and nodded and motioned to me to step forward.

"One of Billy's playmates . . . ah, friends . . . " the priest caught himself as I walked over and stood next to him. " . . . one of Billy's friends has composed a poem in remembrance of him, and he will read it for us now."

I saw a couple of shrugged shoulders among a couple of friends, but otherwise I was too nervous to look at anyone—except for Leona that is, who stood there with her eyes cast downward, her dark veil briefly aflutter in a sudden gust of cold wind. I knew she would not look at me. In her black dress, standing so solemn and serene between her parents and the parents of Billy, the scene looked for a moment like a negative of a bride's photograph.

"Elegy . . . " I began, then, knowing that many of my friends and who knows how many others would be confused by the word, I added, " . . . Burial Poem for Billy."

I had practiced reading the poem at least a dozen times in the mirror the previous night. Apparently my dad wrote it for an uncle named Joe—and that's the only part I had to change in copying it over—inserting *Billy*. I felt my voice tremble as I started. From the corner of my eye I saw Danny discreetly shaking his fist with his thumb up. I took a deep breath and read my father's poem—which everyone thought, of course, was mine:

> We step firmly, but with care
> over the soil of this life.
> It is the breath we take
> that brings everything to the surface,
> trees, springs, voices . . .
> Under us, within us, roots strengthen
> until we move among each other
> with grace and respect.
>
> You are there, Billy, standing
> at the edge of a field,
> the sun rising over your shoulder as we shade
>   our eyes
> from the loving light.
>
> It is the wind's strange dance
> that brings us together,
> seeds blown across continents,
> rivers of desire making their way
> through dark, darker interiors.
> What we end up knowing is so little, so loving:
> that we have had each other's company,
> and that is what we cherish in the world.

What can anyone ask for
except a modest acre of the sky to
plant his hopes, a simple blossoming
of stars to guide us . . .
You are there Billy, standing
at the edge of a field,
the sun rising over your shoulder
as we shade our eyes
from the loving light.

It wasn't Billy's mother's gush of tears that brought tears to my eyes as I finished, nor was it Leona's refusal to even glance at me, nor was it, to be honest, the thought of poor Billy himself, a few feet away, cold and motionless in the expensive coffin. I was thinking, strangely enough, of the fact that *that* was the first time anyone, any group of people, ever heard something that my father had written. And nobody except me knew that it was his even then.

"Lovely poem, lovely," whispered the priest as he gently guided me back to my friends. "Thank you, son, I'm sure Billy enjoyed it."

Even if Billy *could* hear it, which I didn't believe, I thought to myself, he would have ridiculed it.

Danny shook my hand, and Cos gave me an affectionate punch in the arm. Carm came over in his expensive grey tweed suit:

"Nice Bright Boy . . . beautiful," he shook my hand, manly, gentlemanly, "you're a talented sonofabitch."

They lowered the coffin into the ground. Mr. Falvo passed out flowers from the sympathy arrangements and people walked over and threw them onto the casket. Mike, Billy's closest friend, broke down for a moment, but when we tried to comfort him he pushed us away and said he was fine. Leona lifted her veil and kissed a rose before tossing it into the grave. I had to turn away from that. A few more people, some whom I did not recognize, complimented me on the poem—two people even asked if they could get a copy of it. Johnny Pops motioned for us to get going. I picked up a carnation from the ground and walked over and tossed it on Billy's casket. I forgave him for the push he gave me in front of the ice cream parlor. I pictured him doing his backflip in front of the house—I would have included that, I thought, in any poem I had written for him. "So long, Billy," I found myself saying, two big tears running down my face.

I took a last look at Leona in black. She was opening the door of her father's car. I knew that from that time on I didn't have to compete anymore with a handsome, All-American type for the affections of the girl I loved; instead I had to compete the rest of my life with a goddamn saint!

. . . On the way home, in Johnny Pops' Dodge, the smell we had noticed earlier and had blamed on both the fumes of the procession and, as Mike said, the proximity of *tutsoonies*, got worse.

"Jesus," said Danny, holding his nose, "whoever's blowin' it out that bad, "and nodding toward Dutch, " better go see a fuckin' doctor."

"Open the window," gagged Mike, his eyes still red from crying. "Smells more like a dead animal," said Johnny, leaning his head out the window as he drove.

He was right, that's what it smelled like. And at that moment it struck me: the dead rats Cosmo was carrying in a bag several nights earlier. He never did explain it to me. I looked at him, and he winked. Of course I didn't say a word as we drove home—though I knew somewhere in Johnny's car were stashed a couple of dead, rotting rats.

PART TWO
*
Sled Run

CHAPTER VI

The day after Billy's funeral it began to snow. Less than an inch covered the neighborhood, but it was enough to put us back in the right frame of mind for the season. The hill at the end of Cummings Street with its rotted elm dark against the winter sky was the first place we'd abandon in the cold weather. Eventually Jack would throw us out of the Mobil station too—there was hardly enough room for a couple of customers in the place let alone four or five rambunctious teenagers. So from mid-November on we spent a lot more time sipping cokes, eating tripe and pizza, and just hanging out at the *Bay & Goodman Grill*.

About two weeks earlier, the stink finally left Johnny Pops' father's Dodge. He was fit to be tied—and we all tried to avoid Johnny when he was in a bad mood. I tried especially to avoid Johnny, because I was sure he didn't like the idea that I was helping out with Sled Run.

Indeed, Danny, me, and Cosmo had a right to stay away from Johnny, since we were the only ones who knew how the dead rats got deep into the fender walls through the trunk of his car.

"Cos," I said, the afternoon of Billy's funeral, "Cos, you didn't . . . tell me you didn't?" I felt that knowing grin grace my lips, and Cosmo grinned sheepishly in return.

"I had to Rosey," he said, finally with a burst of confession. "It was something I just had to do—like the voice telling me to do it."

"A voice telling you?" I questioned him, "to stuff rats, dead rats in the fender walls of Johnny's father's car?" "Well," replied Cosmo, correcting me, "the voice actually told me to stuff dead *cats* into the car—I guess the rats were my idea."

We told Danny, of course, who must have laughed for half an hour—as did we. Cos admitted that it was repayment for that night on the hill when Johnny forced him to light the tail of old Lady Reilly's cat. One night, in fact, Johnny pulled me aside at the Bay & Goodman Grill and asked me in a whisper if I knew anything about it—and even asked if I thought Cosmo had anything to do with it. Johnny wasn't quite dumb as we thought. I told him I didn't know anything about it.

From then on anytime something smelled, somebody farting, Cosmo's mother's cooked cabbage, or even the back brakes on Mike's Chevy, someone would say "smells like a rat—where's Johnny." And we all had a laugh. Danny, Cos and I would look at each other and share a secret laugh as an encore.

My sister Lonnie became the first kid in the neighborhood or from either of my parents' families in fact to apply for college—the State College of Geneseo, about forty miles from Rochester, but another world in our minds. My father was meticulous in his examination of the application. He had Lonnie rewrite the paragraph she had to include five times! Judy, clearly brighter than Lonnie and I put together, asked Lonnie and my dad if they wanted her to write it for them—"I've got ten minutes with nothing to do," she said in her sarcastic manner. It would not surprise us, later on in life, to see Judy go through the best schools, graduating *magna cum laude*, and getting a graduate degree without my parents ever paying for a day of her education.

But Lonnie, nevertheless, was the first. And we were all excited for her, because, of course, it was our own possibilities we were witnessing. My mother, in her worrisome way, argued against it because of the expenses. But my father, in his true manner, replied, "Let's just get her in first—then we can worry." Lonnie, meanwhile, in the spirit of her new adventure, brought more homework from school every night and, I noticed, held her books a little higher under her arms, a little more deliberate. How quickly, it would always amaze me, people assume roles when possibilities seem real.

But for Mary Kay, Danny's beautiful, sexy sister, it was a different story. In fact, the week before Thanksgiving she quit school. She had never been a very good student—but then how many were in East High's graduating class of 300 or so? And why did a model, or an actress, or a beauty queen have to worry about marks and school in general?

" . . . she might get married—I don't know—she's not much for school anyway," said Danny in a subdued voice, shrugging his shoulders, obviously not wanting to discuss it.

"Married!" said Mike, incredulously, "To who?" His disbelief was ours—because none of us could equate glamour of Mary Kay's magnitude with *marriage*. Especially since—to everyone's bewilderment—she had been dating, of all people, short, chubby, homely Little Christo for the past month or two. So we all strained our ears sitting there at the corner of the *Bay & Goodman Grill* and waited for the answers we did not want to hear.

"Maybe . . . maybe Little Christo," Danny mumbled, obviously embarrassed himself over such an utterance of a potential brother-in-law. In fact it was Danny a couple of weeks earlier who had described Little Christo as "a bubble of a man with a permanent five o'clock shadow."

"She does what she wants," said Danny through a mouthful of tripe, "I don't give a shit, so let's forget it."

I don't know if the image of California and Mary Kay clad in her short white shorts strolling down some sunny street came to anyone's mind, but it did mine. Nobody said anything about California though, and neither did I. Mike farted and sure enough Danny took a big sniff and rolled his eyes: "Jesus," he said, "rats— I'd know it anywhere. Where's Johnny?"

* * *

"Goddamn cold," said Carm, blowing into his wool knit gloves as he got out of the car and pulled the seat back to let me out of the back, "a heat wave one week, a blizzard the next—only in Rochester," he griped.

The snow arrived early in November and stayed. A month earlier there was talk of an exceptionally mild winter and fluctuating wind streams suggesting some cosmic activity and another ice age. Now the local T.V. weathermen began leafing through the *Farmer's Almanac* and quoting from it in front of their incomprehensible maps sprinkled with temperature readings. Yes, they suddenly changed their assessment—a big, bad, Rochester winter ahead.

"A good thing these guys aren't in charge of garbage collection," said my father, shaking his head as he sat in his imitation leather recliner lounge in front of the television, "we'd be in *funky* trouble." My father was the first person whom I ever heard use the word *funky*—and the last person I ever heard use it correctly, meaning having an offensive odor. It wasn't that he was *chic*, of course—just of those trend-setters that sinks into anonymity before anyone picks up on anything . . .

It was our second Sled Run in as many nights. Curley, the big muscle bound heavy, was with us as he had been the previous night. On this second night Bambi joined us as well. I was a little nervous because Bambi and Curley were such tough dudes I assumed whenever they were asked to be somewhere, trouble was expected.

The previous night had been as smooth as the icicles we chipped away from the back window—which obviously had been left open for us. We passed the boxes through the window—twenty of them, good size, about three feet long and heavy. "You've got to eat a little more steak," said Carm, seeing me struggle with one of them as we placed them into the back of the van. One box slipped from my hand and wedged against the back bumper, ripping open a little. I saw the initials *N.H.L.* on the inner box, and pushing the ripped cardboard aside I saw the rest of the print: *N.H.L.* Hockey Action. "Jesus, Carm," I exclaimed, sounding a little younger than my sixteen years, and certainly younger than a professional thief, "hockey games!"

I had asked for one on the Christmas before, but they were too expensive for my dad to afford. They had been out only a couple of years earlier, and I'd played it twice at one of my cousin's friend's house. I still wanted one, but they were still expensive, and anyhow, my dad said he'd buy me a pair of ice skates—and that, I thought to myself, was the real thing.

I guess it was the way I said "hockey games," the excitement in my voice and all, and the way I kept looking it over on the way home in the van as we dropped off Curley that made Carm do it. But as Carm left me off at Jack's darkened gas station, he pulled out the ripped box and said, "here, maybe you know someone who could use one of these. Anyhow, we don't deal with damaged merchandise, right," and he looked over and winked at Bambi and then smiled at me as he handed it over. "Goodnight, Bright Boy . . . see ya tomorrow night."

I'm not sure how I felt as I lumbered home and hid the hockey game in my cellar. First of all, I'd have to explain it to my father, and that bothered me because I'd have to lie directly to him. I didn't mind indirect lies, the kind where you leave out a detail, or omit something, or exaggerate or understate. Misleading was one thing, an art that had more to do with one's fantasies more than an outright falsehood. But an all-out lie—especially to someone who loved and trusted you—was, in my mind, unpardonable.

The other thing that bothered me was that if I actually took something myself, the Sled Run, at least in part, would be tainted. It wouldn't be charity, which the others and I saw it as, it would be plain, simple, petty thievery. It would question the integrity of the entire Sled Run operation, and I did not want to ask myself too many questions about that.

But then how I loved twisting and pulling on those levers, making the players skate and dance and slice at the small rubber puck over the ice-skate metal of the miniature rink. I hid it behind some old snow tires that my father didn't use anymore. I'd decide how to explain it later.

* * *

We picked up Bambi in front of the *Bay & Goodman Grill* where he was waiting for us. Then he drove up Goodman Street to *Skinny's* to pick up Curley. He hopped in the van with a couple of orders of steamed clams, which he must have finished before the traffic light changed on the corner.

"Gabe must know I'm in on this," said Curley as we drove down Norton Street toward the warehouse, "cause he winked at me just now at *Skinny's*."

"Maybe he's trying to pick you up," Bambi tried to laugh but it turned into a cough. "Gotta get rid of these someday," he said, looking at his lit cigarette.

"Gabe in *Skinny's*?" Carm asked.

"Just saw 'em a minute ago," replied Curley.

"Probably thinks he's establishing an alibi," laughed Carm, his teeth gleaming under the passing streetlights.

"What a wimp," added Bambi; then turning to Carm, "why'd you use him Carm—I mean the guy's a fucken' wimp."

"Who else do you know that works there Bambi?" Who else is gonna leave the window open and shut off the alarm for us?"

"All right . . . okay—but I still I think the guy's a wimp Carm."

We parked behind the warehouse just off Norton Street. I started to get out of the van with the others, but Carm held his hand up against the door.

"Stay here Bright Boy—just transistor radios, we don't need a couple of us. We'll be out in a minute."

Sure enough the window was open, and the three of them scampered through. I wasn't watching more than five minutes when the cop car pulled around back and parked at the other end of the building, where the delivery doors were located. I ducked and caught my breath before inching up to look out the van window. The policeman got out and walked over to the doors. My first instinct was to yell out Carm's name, like I did the past summer when the *Fiz* pop man was coming back to his truck and Danny was up on top stealing a couple of quarts of crème soda. But I suppressed it, and instead—as if my body were reacting before my mind came to any conclusions—slipped out the driver's door, which was left ajar. Crouched down, sure the policeman couldn't see me from that angle in the dark, I ran over to the open window and crawled in.

I ran down the first row of boxes I came to. There was enough light from a couple of night lights here and there to see where you were going, but not much else. The first row seemed to go on forever—and I didn't see or hear anyone. I crawled over a box and made my way to the next row, which I ran down trying to be as quiet as I could. Still, no Carm, no Bambi, no Curley. At the end of that row, I quickly turned up the next, and before I knew what happened, I felt someone's arm slam against my face and my arm bent painfully behind me against my back. I might have yelled, but my mouth was covered by a huge hand. When I opened my eyes, I saw with relief, Carm's face in front of mine, his hand holding a pistol and that smile suddenly spreading across his shadowed face. "Easy, Bright Boy," he whispered, "we didn't know it was you."

"A cop," I gasped, Curley's hand suddenly pulled away from my mouth, " . . . there's a cop outside Carm," I said, gasping for my breath.

Carm led us down one of the rows, one hand behind his back motioning to us, the other still holding a pistol. From behind several boxes we could see the window through which we had entered. There was a silhouette of someone in the glass, and from the shape of his hat it was the cop.

"Shhh . . . " said Carm, holding his finger to his lips.

"Fucken' Gabe," whispered Bambi over my shoulder, "he's a fuck-up, I told ya."

The next thing that happened surprised all of us. From the hush of our own fear, in the silent echo of the empty warehouse, a voice rang out, clear, clear and calm, as if we were sitting on the hill next to the gas station.

"Carm, Carm," the voice carried through the warehouse. "Carm . . . is that you? It's Phil—you gotta get out of here quick, there's another squad car on the way . . . "

We jumped out of the window and rushed into the van. We didn't say anything to Phil, Carm's brother, as he walked elegantly in his uniform toward the locked delivery doors, purposely ignoring us. For a moment, though, as we passed him, I saw him exchange looks with Carm—"the alarm," he said softly, "be careful."

As we pulled out of the parking lot and onto Norton Street, we saw two police cars with their sirens and flashers going down Hudson Avenue.

Nobody said anything for a couple of minutes.

"Close, huh?" sighed Bambi, lighting a cigarette. "That goddamn Gabe. I told ya . . . "

"Shut up," roared Carm—and even Bambi, the roughest of the bunch, didn't say a word.

At *Skinny's*, Carm told Curley and Bambi to go in and get Gabe. "Be a pleasure . . . " said Bambi, as he slammed the door shut.

"What happened, Carm?" I asked, hoping a few words might ease the tension I felt in the van.

"The creep didn't shut off the alarm," he said, staring straight ahead. "He didn't do his job, that's all," he went on, calmly—but I could feel the anger welling in his throat.

"Lucky, huh, it was Phil who showed up . . . "

"Yea," he replied, "lucky for Phil."

Gabe, whom I had seen before at the *Bay & Goodman Grill* occasionally, was as white as a ghost as he stumbled between Bambi and Curley on the way to the van. Curley had his huge hand on the back of Gabe's neck, and it looked like he was using some force. Carm jumped out of the driver's seat and ran to the back of the van and opened the doors. "Back here guys," he said, and by that time Bambi and Curley seemed to be dragging Gabe.

"What's wrong Carm?" Gabe said with a shaky, high-pitched voice, "Carm, wait . . . "

As they pushed him into the van, Carm motioned for me to get out. He then turned to me and handed me a dollar bill. "Get me a coffee to go," he said, nodding toward the restaurant.

Perhaps I should have known to take a little more time, but with the coffee in my hand I stood next to the van. Apparently, they had not finished with him yet, and from the inside the van came a few muffled sounds and then a couple of deep grunts. I imagined the thin, pale Gabe doubled-up with Curley standing over him, his huge fist coiled. I tried not to picture Carm, although I knew of the three, Carm was the one seething.

When Carm came out of the back of the van, he brushed himself off, as one might when stepping in from a snowstorm. On his knuckles, as I handed him the coffee, I noticed blood. He looked at the blood, then at me, and that old big grin came to his lips.

"When things go wrong, everybody gets hurt," he said, putting his hand on my shoulder. I looked in the van, and Gabe was on his knees, head down, wiping his bloodied face with his light grey wool overcoat. When he looked up and our eyes met, I had to turn away. It looked like his whole face had been split open. It was already puffed and darkened. I walked up to the front of the van, repressing the urge I felt to vomit.

* * *

Still feeling ill, I went straight upstairs, grunting as articulate a *goodnight* as I could to my mother and father who sat in the kitchen having their coffee nightcap. My sister Judy came out of the bathroom as I reached the top of the stairs—"Too much to drink?" she said, sarcastically, as she took a look at me.

"Fuck you," I mumbled, making my way to my room.

"Ah, the poet in the family . . . " I heard her say as she closed the door to her bedroom.

I quickly undressed and got into bed. They had left Gabe in the parking lot hunched against a pick-up truck. Carm gave him the coffee. One last look at the guy as we pulled away made me nauseous all over again. I tried to get his beaten face out of my mind as I lay there in my bed, but every time I closed my eyes the image grew more clear. One line from one of my father's poems kept running through me—*inside the scar on the face of a stranger . . . Gabe's* face appeared again. It struck me that one mistake, one, and a man sees himself distorted, disfigured, for the rest of his life.

It must have been five minutes, perhaps ten, when I got up and, without disturbing anyone—my mom and dad were still downstairs in the kitchen—quickly made my way to the closet in my parents' bedroom. I took out the old notebooks and brought them back to my bed. I turned on the Howdy Doody lamp on my nightstand—my parents had never replaced it.

I had remembered a number of poems that made me curious since there seemed to be beneath the surface an underlying violence that I couldn't connect to my father's calm, easy-going manner. But he *did* box as a young man—to which Danny's father could attest (but never would I was sure). And every Wednesday and Friday nights at ten o'clock he watched the boxing matches on television, moving his fists and even standing up when someone was on the verge of a knockdown. I found a couple of poems immediately—one that struck me as a beauty the first time I read it, though I could not picture my father robbing a gas station. It was titled, that bold, elegant printing above the scribbled verse, "On Some Nights." I read it to myself, but halfway through found myself saying the words aloud—

> . . . and when the light above me
> grows dim with my boredom,
> I close the book, and stand up
> all by myself
> ready now for the gun.
> But just as I imagine
> the attendant unconscious and the cash register
> open beside him,
> a voice runs through me like the most distant
> of sirens,
> a wife's request:
> that I sit at her bedside and watch her fall asleep.
> I do.
> She does.
> My knuckles break the silence
> that collects in the hands.

There was something chilling about that poem. I couldn't imagine my mother asking my father to sit at her bedside, and I couldn't imagine my father *holding* a gun let alone using one. But somehow the potential of some deep violent eruption, even in the setting of the material bedroom, seemed credible. As I lay there, I couldn't help thinking that Carm's anger that night, the knee that he probably lifted into Gabe's chest, the fist he may have smashed into his face, was the ultimate expression of some steady, even-paced assessment that someone like my father might have made in a calmer moment at another time in the neighborhood. I read on—another poem from the notebook:

> " . . . so what do I do
> with this switchblade I fondle
> with idle hands as I walk through this idle life.
> Behind me, in the shadows
> of my own making,
> I leave behind memory,
> which follows at a distance expecting to be led
> to treasure or crime, I don't
> know which . . ."

The neighborhood, it struck me that night, was a collective. Not just the mechanic and the baker, the priest and the garbage-man, but the thinker, the spokesman, the dreamer, the realist, the victim and the enforcer. We were all a part of something that de-fined us as a group. Everything fit—from the smell of the dead rats in Johnny's Dodge to the first wrapped gifts for the orphans. From Billy's meaningless death to Phil Carlotta's allegiance to his friends. From Leona's lovely smile to Gabe's bloodied nose. The question we would ask ourselves, would continue asking ourselves for many years to come, would be, *how did we all fit in?* I looked at the po-em, felt the dust on my seemingly innocent fingertips as I turned the page of the notebook. These poems, it occurred to me—abandoned, precious, never to be read—might be as essential to my world as Carm's red Mercury convertible. I read on, finally finding the poem I'd been looking for—

> " . . . and in this room filled
> with a hundred acquaintances,
> the old joke's been forgotten . . .
> But still the elbow pokes at the ribs of
> the humorless

until a wound appears.
From it seeps something like blood,
and we're reminded of a childhood incident,
    and look around,
bewildered again,
until we see the scar on the face of a stranger
among us,
where so much pain is being kept from
    the world."

* * *

I woke up with the sun streaking across the faint dust of my bedroom and the notebook still resting on my chest. It had been one of those exhaustive, restful sleeps—dream upon distinct and yet immemorable dream, until one awakens with the mind clear and the body empty. I glanced at the clock and was sorry to see it was almost eight. I thought for a moment of feigning a cold and skipping school; but when my father appeared at my doorway and asked me to see him at breakfast, I decided I'd better not.

He handed me a twenty dollar bill as I sat at the kitchen table. "This is for gifts for your mom and your sisters," he said, pressing it into my hand. "Get them something nice." Actually, there was something else he wanted to ask about. He found the hockey game behind the old snow tires in the cellar. "Who's it for, Rosey? You buy it?'"

"Carm Carlotta gave it to me, dad."

"Where'd he get it?"

"From someone . . . from somewhere. I'm not sure."

"Is it stolen Rosey?" My father had a way of casually coming right to the heart of the matter.

"I don't know," I lied.

"Nobody give things away Rosey. Especially a guy like Carm."

"What do you mean dad, Carm's given me a lot of things—like the wax I used to do your car last summer . . . "

"You know what I mean son. That hockey game is brand new—and expensive. Carm didn't buy it to give to you or anyone. I doubt very much if he bought it. What do you think?"

"I don't know."

"Did it ever cross your mind?"

"Well . . . "

"Well?" he asked again.

"Yea, I guess so."

"And what did you come up with, Rosey?"

It was a typical talk with my father. He would never lecture to us—he'd ask questions until we were forced to utter what we knew or felt or thought was the right judgment. I knew what was coming, and I couldn't argue with it. I stashed the twenty dollar bill in my pocket and, taking a last sip of coffee, promised to give the hockey game back to Carm. That too was a lie, but not a total lie.

That afternoon, after school, I gave the hockey game to Danny. I snuck into his house (at least I felt that way since Danny's dad wouldn't allow me inside the house) and we screamed and groaned while the plastic puck flew into each other's plastic nets until half an hour before his father was due home. Mary Kay didn't say anything about me being there, and in turn, we didn't say anything (except an exchange of knowing smiles between us) when she disappeared with Little Christo into her bedroom for a while. I tried not to think of what they might have been doing.

CHAPTER VIII

It was two weeks before Christmas. The snow was here to stay—enough of the white stuff and cold to make up for the unusually hot October—which, of course, with Billy's absence, was still warm in our minds. And that posed for me a serious question concerning the season: whether or not to give Leona a Christmas gift?

I knew by heart each place and time I might see her during the day. I knew which bus she took, what table she ate lunch at, and even what hallways she might pass through on her way to classes. She spoke to me of course, said hello, smiled, and even asked me to read over a book report she wrote because she had read only half the book. But that was just it—the normality was just killing me. I had to know what she felt inside. I could still taste her lips from the night of what I would call for years "the fatal kiss."

Mr. Penfield, meanwhile, assigned us another of his imaginative essays for English class: *The Meaning of Christmas*. I put my hand over my eyes as he announced the theme, and in the row across from me Cosmo held his nose between his fingers. The essay was the "take home" type, a new method teachers were using, one which wasn't too bad because you could get someone to help you, but one which necessitated a lot of time and energy away from school—which pissed off most of us.

"Let's give him something he won't forget Rosey," said my sister Judy when I showed her Mr. Penfield's assignment. "Come on," she smiled, "I'll help you." I should have known by that devious look—that my paper was the perfect place for her to exercise her clever, mischievous mind. And I would have done it on my own except that Danny's father was out that night and we had the chance to play with the hockey game, and the next night was the last Sled Run of the season with Carm and his companions—to pick up, he informed me confidentially, a batch of portable radios at an electronics warehouse. We finished the essay in less than an hour. Once I got into the mood of Judy's wit, I even wrote a couple of sentences myself, which, according to my smart sister, gave me the right to call my essay a *composite*, if asked—whatever that meant.

The Meaning of Christmas
by Rosey Tarcone

I guess if we were honest it wouldn't be difficult to state the true meaning of Christmas—lots of lights, flights of materialistic fantasies, higher prices, huge department stores profits, bankrupt savings accounts, and a joyous spirit equaled only by its accompanying depression. It's a fact that suicides rise as the holy spirit descends upon us.

Of course we're not supposed to say these things. I guess we're supposed to see beyond ourselves and answer the question, "In the best of both worlds, what is the meaning of Christmas?" Wait. That's not right either. How about, "In the best of Christian worlds, what is the meaning of Christmas?"

My answer: I don't know. And I don't think I'm alone in my ignorance. As a famous twentieth-century poet wrote (I showed Judy a copy of my father's poem, but I didn't tell her it was his), "my blood flows for an answer"—which is a nice way of saying we must live in order to learn. Being an atheist, I have a tough time dealing with this time of the year.

But as a sophomore in high school, I understand symbolism. I guess the Miracle Birth should remind us that there's a spirit within us more powerful and amazing than out biological being. Add to that that God's gift is an ultimate sacrifice—the giving of his only son to this world—and one might get the idea that the season has to do with unselfishness, charity and hope.

Not as I see it. No way. From what I can tell, Christmas is a Capitalistic Dream. What better way is there to equate material goods with good feelings? Give me a consumer singing "Joy to the

World," and I'll lay odds behind him there's a manufacturer and a retailer harmonizing in a choral procession all the snowy, star-twinkling way to the bank.

To me, the meaning of Christmas in America has to do with inventiveness: how we transformed a holy day into the light-blinking, tinsel hanging, gut-filling celebration that justifies our greed.

Finally, sometimes I think it's better not to ask such questions. Once in a while, no answer is better than the truth.

* * *

The temperature rose the next afternoon, and after school we began throwing snowballs at Jack's gas station. We'd bet a nickel a vehicle, the object being to hit the first vowel of the first word of whatever was printed on the side. For instance, City Transit on the side of the bus meant the first person to hit the *i* in the *City* collected a nickel from everyone. Billy had always been the best shot, winning as much as five dollars in an afternoon. After his death, it was between Danny and me. We had been throwing snowballs for about an hour when Mary Kay walked past on her way home. Even in the winter she was gorgeous, her shapely body showing more through her tight, black snow-pants, her perfect, delicate face more pronounced surrounded by the blue and white wool ski hat. Her graceful solitude always made us stop whatever we were doing for a moment. But now it was something more—the idea that she had been seduced and won over by someone shorter, pudgier, and less handsome than ourselves made us uneasy. A *Schwalb Oil* truck passed and no one tossed a snowball at it. It was only a matter of time when the uneasiness of the quick looks to each other, the sudden clearing of throats, would turn to a few chosen words, even in the presence of her brother Danny.

It was Dutch who broke the silence—and despite his being older and bigger than Danny, he paid for it dearly. It might have been any of us, to tell the truth, who may have uttered what at heart was our own disillusion. Mary Kay had represented to us a potential escape into a glamorous life, and when she became in our eyes no more than some neighborhood slob's wife, we were ready to blame her for it—to ridicule her as we might have our own ambitions. In touch with the world as we were, we were not especially kind.

I don't remember, to be truthful, what Dutch said as we stood there packing our small, hard snowballs. In the midst of Dutch's hyena laughter I think I heard the word *bride* followed by some undecipherable grunt. Maybe Danny didn't hear it either, but I don't think it mattered much.

Danny tossed his gloves away like a hockey player and lunged toward Dutch with a right that looked like Marciano's. It landed too, echo of bone on bone distinct in the clear winter air. Dutch went down in agony and by the time he pulled his hand away from his eye it was already black and blue. After a moment or so he was standing and making the usual verbal threats toward Danny. But I could tell after seeing Danny throw that right hand that he'd no longer have to worry about threats from Dutch—nor from me or Cosmo, and maybe even from Mike after that time on. "He had it comin'," I whispered to him.

Mary Kay never looked back. She disappeared down Cumming Street as usual, even with all the commotion. It seems the solitude she had instilled in us each time she passed as we found ourselves speechless, had made its way into her own heart—a heart, Danny would tell Cosmo and me that night, that was beating for two.

* * *

I think it was the letter from the newspaper, my poem . . . well, my father's poem that is, that gave me courage to approach Leona and tell her, or at least attempt to tell her, how I felt.

It was waiting for me when I got home after Danny came of age and blackened Dutch's eye. I had forgotten about the contest, the annual competition sponsored by a suspicious sounding group: *Friends of the Library*. I guess it was the coincidence: discovering my father's poems, especially the one about Christmas, and reading about the contest for the best seasonal poem by a high school student. If I thought I had a chance, I would have changed a few words here and there, instead of sending the poem, *verbatim*—with my name, age, school, and my English teacher's name, Mr. Penfield, attached to it.

Not only had I won a twenty-five dollar government savings bond, but my poem . . . well, *the* poem . . . would be published in the newspaper on Christmas Day. A photographer from the *Democrat & Chronicle* would come to my house and take a photo which would accompany the poem. On the bottom of the official notification was a handwritten note: *this is a beautiful, sophisticated lyric. Congratulations, you are a talented young man.*

My sisters made me show them the letter. They were amazed. They read too the copy of the poem the Friends of the Library had attached to the letter. They were even more amazed.

"Okay, gator-brain," said Judy, looking at me and shaking her head, "where did my illiterate brother find this poem?"

"You don't think I wrote it?" I mumbled, looking away.

"Just because we love you Rosey," said Lonnie in her warm, disarming way, "doesn't mean *we don't know you.*"

"You're jealous," I snapped at both of them. That brought a grin to my face, and I couldn't restrain it.

"Come on," Judy implored after we all had a good laugh, "where'd you find the poem Rosey?" I decided to amaze them even more.

"Dad . . . "

Their eyes opened wide, and puzzled looks came across their faces.

"Dad wrote it," I continued. "He wrote it and a hundred more poems—and they're upstairs in his closet, and they're . . . well, they're really something . . . "

"This I gotta see," said Judy, already making her way up the hallway stairs.

I'll never forget that night. We all sat in the kitchen table passing the notebook around reading aloud my father's poems. He even read a few. I thought he'd be mad because I said I wouldn't say anything about them—and obviously my mother must have promised she wouldn't either. But he wasn't a bit angered, or embarrassed, or saddened. After Judy read one, a stunning, moving poem about leaving home (had that been on his mind?) which ended,

> . . . .the instinctive turn
> toward the wind that touches,
> equally, both shoulders,
> both minds.

My father's eyes seemed to glaze over as he looked at us with his warm, wonderful smile.

"You know," he said, grabbing my hand and Judy's on either side of him, "I've waited almost thirty years to discover why I spent so much time and energy writing these things that nobody ever gave me a goddamn care in the world about—and tonight, here, with you, now I know why they were written." My mother sniffed into a dishtowel, tears in her eyes.

"But what about the Christmas poem," asked Judy a few minutes later, "and Rosey's bogus award? It's not right Dad—you wrote it, why should he get the credit?"

I put my head down, feeling absolutely ashamed. Judy was right.

"That's plagiarism, isn't it Dad?" asked Lonnie.

"It's not that bad girls," my mother came to my defense. Then she added with her special wisdom, "it's all in the family at least."

We turned to my father who seemed hesitant to say anything. He took a breath and started to say something after giving me a stern but loving look. But at that moment the doorbell rang. It was the photographer from the newspaper.

* * *

I rushed through the lunch line at school. Leona's friends always joined her several minutes after she sat down, and that afternoon I was determined to join her before they showed up.

I was feeling especially high-spirited because of the previous night. When the photographer had announced who he was and started unbuckling and spreading out his photographic gear, I thought my father was going to send him away, proclaiming that some mistake had been made and that we were withdrawing the poem from the contest.

But he did not.

He even suggested his big imitation leather lounge chair for the picture, but the photographer decided on the glass-covered maple desk (which we never used) in the dining room. He had me pose with a pencil and a piece of paper, making me look like the writer I was supposed to be. He also had me pose with my hands ignorantly on the keys of Judy's typewriter, and for a moment I felt like a real writer. "Do you want me to bring down your notebook of poems Rosey?" Judy asked in an amazingly sweet and sickening voice. Lonnie turned her laughter into a coughing spell and rushed into the other room.

Afterwards, when the photographer had left, my father explained his countenance. "I guess it's a matter of weighing the right and wrong. It's wrong to be deceitful, Rosey, especially claiming to have done something aesthetic and distinctive. But I trust you know that. On the other hand," and at that point he looked at all of us and smiled, "the poem deserves to be read by more than five of us in this household. I wish my name was under it, but let's face it—it's only being published as a result of a curious, adolescent whim. It's just by chance that it's a serious piece of writing . . . "

Judy shrugged her shoulder and made a face. But she didn't disagree; it was her respect for my father and his keen, kind mind that drove her to be the intellectual she was becoming.

" . . . but best of all," my father continued, "this will put some pressure on Rosey. His teachers will expect to see more good writing now, right?" he nodded to me and brushed his hand playfully through my hair.

He made me promise to send the newspaper a poem for Easter as a follow-up—one I would do strictly on my own, not even a phrase from one of his poems or any others for that matter. I agreed to do so.

" . . . so what's up Rosey?" Leona tore open a bag of *Cheez-its* and sipped her coke. That was her normal fare for lunch.

To tell the truth, she never acted hostile or moody anytime we said anything in passing. I was the one with the nagging conscience, the guilt, the strange feeling of some kind of betrayal. Perhaps, I thought, I was manufacturing some good, solid, legitimate reasons for rejection, because simple rejection by itself was potentially too devastating, too universal to accept.

"Oh, nothing much," I answered, trying to achieve some casual tone, "I just won a poetry contest in the *Democrat & Chronicle*." I guess I wanted her respect right away.

"Poetry? You, Rosey?"

"Yea, it'll be in the Christmas morning newspaper, photo too."

"Poetry? You know, I wrote some after Billy's death—I'd never written anything like that before. But," she added, "I'll never show them to anyone—I keep them locked up in a nightstand drawer."

Great. Not one minute into the conversation and somehow I found a way for her to bring up Billy. Her *nightstand*, I thought, *a sanctuary of dreams!* For a moment I pictured her in some silky nightgown, head propped back against a pillow, her hair still a little damp from the shower—and with a lovely, ceremonious yawn, reaching to her nightstand drawer and pulling out a poem about Billy, like a nighttime prayer—*Now I lay me down to sleep, Billy, my heart is yours to keep* . . . A couple of sensuous tears falling down her cheeks and touching her lips like some god-sent kiss . . .

"I didn't know you wrote poetry Rosey," she interrupted the image in my mind.

"Well . . . I just started to," I replied, "sort of in the family—my father was a writer."

"Oh really. How interesting."

"Yea . . . " Suddenly I felt I had to legitimize my statement: " . . . published a lot of things when he was young."

"Wow. How exciting. You know," she hesitated, looking as if she had recognized something between us, "my father's in that same business."

"Really?" I had never known what her father did for a living.

"He sets print for the *Catholic Courier*."

I smiled. Little by little I had discovered early on, one learned to keep one's convictions to himself, for the sake of—well, in this case for the sake of romance, which had, in our adolescent minds, nothing to do with any of the issues of ideology or beliefs. Not one atheistic utterance would spill from my lips in the presence of Leona. Another image flashed through my mind: A *Catholic Courier* under my arm with my books, its cover radiating like a beacon against my thumb!

I saw one of Leona's lunch pals moving along the cafeteria line. I had another three or four minutes alone with her, so I had better spit it out. "Leona, I . . . " I took a deep swallow of nothing. "I want to apologize for that night . . . "

"What night Rosey? What are you talking about?"

It surprised me that she didn't know what I was referring to. I wanted to say as little as possible.

"The night . . . the night Billy was, ah . . . "

"Oh, that night," she said solemnly. For a moment she looked down, as if saying a private, momentary grace. The she looked back at me, refreshed, beautiful, bright eyed. "What about it?"

"Well Leona . . . it's . . . what's been bothering me—because your friendship means a lot me—what's been bothering me is that . . . that . . . *that kiss* . . . "

"Kiss?"

"Yea . . . " I didn't want to go into a description. Would she deny it? "The one, between you and me—I mean, you know, when I walked you home—in front of your house . . . "

"Rosey—you kissed me? Then? I was so wiped out by the wine in Cosmo's garage, I don't remember a thing." Then she looked at me curiously: "You didn't kiss me that night, did you?"

Her girlfriend sat down next to Leona as I stuttered for an answer. I was glad she did—because the kiss of death which had haunted me was suddenly in question. Not in my mind, where it was cherished above all else, but in Leona's, where it could have fueled a lifetime of resentment.

I excused myself as another of Leona's friends sat at the table. I knew I had to reassess this relationship. Still, her poem in the drawer of the nightstand seemed more significant than mine (my father's, that is) which would appear in the newspaper.

* * *

To tell the truth, by the night of the last Sled Run before Christmas Eve, I was a little edgy. Down deep, I was hoping Carm would forget about picking me up for this one. But he did, along with our regular crew, Bambi and Curley.

I wish I could have adopted fully Carm's philosophy—that anything was justifiable in the name of the greater good: in this case, the salutation of the gifts to orphans on Christmas Eve. But I kept seeing Gabe's bruised face and hearing his moans' muted echoes in the back of the van. Somehow I couldn't equate all that with charity. On the other hand, I thought, maybe that was a small price to pay for the joy we would bring to those poor kids at St. Joe's and Hillside. Underneath my feelings, I knew and hated to acknowledge, was my father's certain objections to what I was involved in. He had in fact, confirmed his agreement to attend church on Christmas. I didn't know whether that gesture would generate more pleasure for my mother or more disappointment for Judy, my atheist sister, who, in her spark and beliefs, seemed to embody my fa-

ther's feelings about life (but who, to my mother's insistence, at-
tended church herself on major holy days). I had to go, and in fact
enjoyed going to church on Christmas morning because of the pageantry and social spirit of the event, and I looked forward to my
dad being there all dressed up in his brown suit and starched white
shirt, which he wore only to weddings and funerals.

It was a cold night. We pulled into a side street just off Culver
Road past East Avenue. Carm left the van running just to be sure.
There were a few cars in the parking area, but, explained Carm, it
was used by residents of the area to park in at night. Carm had already revealed to me the nature of the merchandise—portable radios—so I was not surprised to see *J & L Electronics Warehouse* printed on a small sign above the entrance. But we did not enter there.
Once again, in a most organized fashion, a door in a darkened corner of the building was conveniently left open for us. We entered
quickly and Bambi turned on his huge flashlight and shined it on a
piece of paper Carm took out of his pocket. It was a hand-drawn
map someone had provided. "Nothing to it," said Carm, motioning to us, "down here."

We made our way down the aisle, Carm alternating the flashlight between map and the numbered, coded boxes stacked on the
shelves. "Right about here if I'm not mistaken," he said to himself,
and just as he reached the shelf he seemed to be looking for, we
heard the commotion.

Of course any noise at all boomed like firecrackers in the echo
of the warehouse—especially in the midst of our own, cautious,
quiet movements. There were the slap of several footsteps, then
what sounded like an avalanche of boxes, and finally a voice:

"Hold it right there . . . Don't move!" Someone spoke authori-
tatively, " . . . easy now, turn around . . . "

We all kneeled in the aisle. But upon hearing the voice again,
Carm got up and started walking toward it. "Shit," he said, "that's
Phil voice.. Sonofabitch." The rest of us looked at each other and
made the sign of the cross, and we too got up and followed Carm.

"Phil . . . Phil . . . " Carm shouted softly, "it's me, Carm; you okay?"

His brother answered him, and when he got to Phil who stood there with his gun drawn and a backup cop behind him, it wasn't just the sight of him that surprised us.

Standing in front of Phil—also with a drawn gun—the two of them facing each other—was none other than Johnny Pops!

We all stood there, eyes wide opened, jaws dropped, not knowing what to say, or think for that matter. Phil and Johnny, old friends, fierce rivals, stood not more than five feet away from each other, their eyes focused intensely on the other's, their hands held in front of them, as if, at another moment, another time, they would shake hands before a boxing match.

"Jesus Christ," exclaimed Carm, shaking his head, standing almost between them. Then he looked at Johnny: "What the hell are you doing here?" Johnny glanced at Carm, but only for a split second as he kept a tense finger on the trigger of his pistol. "You think you're the only one with Christmas spirit?" he said sharply to Carm.

"You mean he's not with you Carm?" Phil asked his brother, surprised.

"No," said Carm.

"I'm not good enough for Sled Run, huh Carm?" Johnny spurt out with a nervous voice. I could see the sweat beading up on his forehead. Phil Carlotta seemed just as nervous, and I wanted to hold my ears, because I knew that a gunshot would explode in a tremendous echo in the warehouse. For a moment I saw them as they stood across each other, end and defensive back on the playground at No. 25 School. They used to battle each other, throwing elbows and shoulders on every play whether or not the play involved them. Now they stood absolutely still, knowing any movement at all might mean a burning hole through the stomach and the absolute end of their adolescent rivalry.

"Carm," said Phil in a quick breath, " get outa here, the alarm went off, we don't have much time." Then he looked at Johnny, "This punk probably set it off with his breath—Go on Carm . . . "

"Forget it Phil," Carm replied sternly, suddenly sitting on a stack of boxes behind him, "I'm not leaving until we all walk out of here together—including Johnny," he seemed to add begrudgingly.

Even in the shadows I could see Phil's white complexion. He stared out at Johnny, who stared back at him. The policeman behind Phil looked even more pale, his hand tense on the gun still in his holster.

"Put the gun down Johnny," Phil said, pleading now.

"Fuck you Phil!" Johnny snapped back, "there's no uniforms between us, we're on the playground Phil—everybody gets bruised, nobody lets go . . . "

"This ain't the playground guys," said Carm, lighting up a cigarette. "If we don't walk out of here in a minute we're all in jail."

"Anybody but Johnny Pops," said Phil, licking his lips, staring straight ahead.

"Me? Look who's wearing the fucking badge."

Carm stood up, and I had the feeling he was going to step between his brother and Johnny, become a hero or a tragedy, but just as he stepped forward, we heard the gunshot.

I guess we all did a double-take—gawking at Johnny, then at Phil, then at Johnny, then at Phil—expecting to see one of them falling over, crumbling at the knees, the gun tumbling out of his hand, a circle of blood spreading outward against the abdomen.

Bu they both stood there, immobilized by the gunshot neither one of them could fire.

"It's Walters," cried out the other policeman, his voice a strange composite of relief and alarm. And when he ran toward the entranceway to the parking lot, we all followed, including Phil and Johnny, their guns dropped to their sides.

I don't know what Walters, the policeman waiting in the parking lot, must have thought as his two comrades ran out of the warehouse along with the five of us, including Johnny with a gun and Curley with an iron pipe he must have found along the way. But he probably didn't waste too much time on the thought, because he was kneeling over, of all things, a deer! There was a good size wound just below his front shoulder, and one look at those huge, glassy, distant eyes as the deer lay there in the snow of the parking lot a few feet from the front tire of our van and I knew it was dying quickly.

"Out of nowhere," said the seemingly ecstatic Walters, "suddenly this deer walks up . . . I mean Phil," he turned to Phil Carlotta, his eyes almost as wide as those of the deer, "I didn't get a shot all deer season this fall, I mean, what could I do?" Then he looked at the rest of us, and he must have remembered suddenly that he was supposed to be looking for a burglary in progress.

"You guys okay?" he asked meekly, adding awkwardly, "these guys with you?"

It was Bambi, who was a seasoned hunter, (thus his nickname), who knelt down and examined the deer. He shook his head, the way he usually did, his pitch black hair falling into his eyes, and I thought he, like all of us, was simply amazed by the last few minutes that had passed—and all of the things, a deer showing up near the corner of Culver and Winston Roads in the middle of Rochester, the timing better than a Hollywood script. But there was something else that amazed him.

"It's not a deer," he announced, as everyone gathered around with stumped expressions on their faces. We looked at the animal, at ourselves, then at Bambi.

"Look at the antlers, low on the brow, and these big, floppy ears," he said, lifting the big round ear in his hand. "Christ," he went on inspecting the dead animal further, "look at the size of this thing—the big chest, the big round hooves, the dew claws. You just bagged yourself one of Santa's best," he said, looking at the confused policeman Walters. "This, gentlemen, is a fucking reindeer!"

Then he rose to his feet and looked around. As a matter of fact we all looked around—and I don't know what everyone else was looking for, because they were much too old to believe in Santa, or for that matter, even in reindeer at Christmas time. And I'm sure I was too old too. But it sure felt weird.

CHAPTER IX

A few days later it was rumored that the policemen in Goodman Street sector had been treated at their Christmas Party to *venizen* steaks compliments of an anonymous donor. So the investigation to the missing reindeer—which had escaped from a small warehouse about a mile from the electronics warehouse—came pretty much to a halt. The promotional sleigh ride down Main Street the following day, sponsored by *Sibley's* department store, bridled up a deer from the Seneca Zoo to complete the foursome needed for the pull.

We had a tough time getting the reindeer into the van. Counting the other policemen that arrived at the warehouse, there must have been fifteen of us pushing, pulling and lifting the dead animal at one time or another. Walters, looking a little pale thinking about the consequences of his kill, kept asking if anyone knew when *reindeer season* ended.

"There isn't any particular season," said Carm, "they're an endangered species."

Someone arranged for us to drop the thing off at a butcher's place on Central Park, and we did—without, Carm had reminded us several times as he cursed out Johnny Pops (who somehow disappeared during the excitement that night), *without* the portable radios.

On the last day of school before Christmas vacation I got back from Mr. Penfield the paper I had "co-authored" with my sister Judy.

Curiously, the paper bore *three* marks on the top of it—two of which were crossed out in the same red marking ink. The first mark was an A, but apparently Mr. Penfield had a change of heart and crossed it out. The next mark was a D, but that too was scribbled out. Finally, he settled on, what else, a C—which in our family circle stood for *commonplace, conventional,* and *cute,* as my father would say. *Well-written but ill-informed,* the English teacher's comment read under the C.

There's a man who doesn't trust his instinct," said Judy upon seeing the paper. Understandably, she took it personal.

But what were Mr. Penfield's instincts, I thought to myself. To reward me for writing well, an *A* for style and use of language? Apparently, at least for a moment or so. Or were his instincts to penalize me for articulating thoughts that seemed ideologically different from some Platonic model spinning in his schematic, assignment-cloning mind? Apparently, because beneath that neurotic scribble was a big fat *D*. The third instinct, the lasting one which would categorize this particular effort (even if it were Judy's) for time-in-memoriam in that little black book of his, was, it struck me, the worst, and represented the weakest link in our national character: to dismiss every bizarre, eccentric, creative and ungodly act by legitimizing it with the normality (and anonymity) of a *C*! For every C on a report card, I remember my father saying, a hundred thousand brain cells die off in cultural suicide.

* * *

I pried out the tacks carefully, trying not to tear the pennant as I removed it from the wall in my bedroom. It was a difficult gift to give up, since not only did I love the Cleveland Browns, but more importantly—and what made that football pennant irreplaceable—Otto Graham, probably the greatest quarterback ever, signed his name across it one night at a promotional event at Alhart's Appliances on Culver Road. And now, in the tradition Danny, Cosmo, and I began several years ago, it would be a Christmas gift—to Danny, who loved football, the Cleveland Browns, and Otto Graham more than I did. How many times he had run his hand over the pennant attached to wall above my bed, saying with a sigh, "Gee, Otto Graham . . . and you shook his hand, you bastard you Rosey . . . "

Every Christmas Eve the three of us, by ourselves, gathered in late afternoon on the hill at the corner and exchanged gifts. At first we exchanged things we already owned because we didn't have any money. But after a couple of exchanges on a couple of Christmases, it became evident our gifts to each other were special because they had meant something already to us, and the sentiment was equal to the sacrifice. I rolled the pennant carefully and wrapped it in the only paper I could find, some powder blue baby shower paper I found in the front closet. Last year, Danny outdid himself—splitting between Cosmo and me the dozen of pornographic photos he had found several days earlier in his father's dresser drawer. "I don't want you guys jerkin' off in my house anymore," he said with his infectious laugh as we opened our gifts leaning against the old, deteriorated half elm on the hill.

It was easier to wrap Cosmo's gift, the red mahogany handled switchblade that had belonged to my grandfather. It was so smooth, and the more you rubbed your hand over it, the more its reddish color seemed to glow from within. Cos had admired it on several occasions, and I had a feeling this gift would please him very much.

That afternoon I rushed over to Danny's house to play the finals of our hockey tournament on the game my father made me give up. We had become, in a short time, pretty good at working the players, our fingers spinning, pushing and pulling on the little knobs. We even replaced the little plastic puck with a black marble to speed up the game. I made my usual entrance into Danny's house, quickly, quietly, and though the back door. I was still banned by his father from being there—but Danny assured me his father would be at work until supper time.

We hadn't finished our first game when we heard the front door slam and his father's gruff voice yell out that he was home. I looked at Danny, watched his jaw drop and his eyes widen. He pointed to the fruit closet, a small, open pantry just off the kitchen, where we had the hockey game set up on the kitchen table. I scrambled into the pantry and hid under a shelf behind an old barrel. Danny went on playing the hockey game, as if he'd been practicing by himself. His father walked in and threw his coat over a chair.

"Where's your sister?" he asked Danny.

"Not here . . . " Danny answered, rocketing the black marble off the side of the miniature rink.

"Well, where is she?"

"I don't know dad, with Christo I guess . . . "

"Shit," his father said with disgust, shrugging his shoulders, "why do I aggravate myself by asking . . . "

He lit a cigarette, and then the pilot of a burner on the stove under a pan of water. "Who's here?" he asked Danny, suspiciously.

"No one dad, just me."

"Rosey hasn't been here?"

"No dad, he's not allowed, remember . . . "

"You'd better."

I could see his dad's work shoes a few feet away in front of me as he mixed his instant coffee at the counter. When he sat at the table, I knew I was in for a long stay under the shelf in the pantry. After a few minutes Danny's father tossed an empty cigarette pack onto the floor. "Quit playing that stupid noisy game and run to the store and get me some *Camels*, huh Danny."

"How about in a little while . . . "

Danny's father pounded his fist on the table so hard the hockey game actually bounced into the air. I closed my eyes, wishing I could disappear.

"*Now* Danny," his father shouted, "when I ask you something, it may sound like a question—but it isn't. It's an order—you got that? Now here . . . " He gave Danny the money, and Danny threw on his coat and left. In that first minute, while Danny's father sat in silence at the table, I held my breath completely. In the next minute or so, it sounded, in my ears at least, as if I were breathing into a microphone. I expected any moment he would tilt his head toward the pantry and raise his hand to his ear, alert to the presence of something alien to the household.

But instead he placed his hands over his face and mumbled something. I think I heard him say Mary Kay's name and mutter something in a disgusted sigh. Then he took a long sip of coffee and held the cup in both hands in front of himself while closing his eyes and hanging his head. It looked like a form of prayer, or meditation, and I had seen that gesture a hundred times, as if another exhausted civilian were blessing the caffeine that manages to keep him going. I looked at the crooked nose, the lasting impression of my father's right hand. I saw the shadows under his eyes, a day's growth of stubble on his stout face. Suddenly I had the impulse (but not the courage) to crawl out of the pantry, walk over to the table, pull back a chair, sit down, and offer Mr. Polito my hand and sympathies. He looked so worn out. It occurred to me as I hid there that it wasn't resentment toward my father or an innate dislike of me that angered and troubled Danny's father. He rubbed his eyes with the huge knuckles of his index fingers.

I heard footsteps and then the door open. I couldn't see the door from the pantry, but I assumed Danny made a record dash to the grocery store for cigarettes, knowing I was trapped in the pantry and not only was my life at stake but Danny's ass as well. But when I saw his father's eyes bulge like bullfrog's and his reddened skin pale in the faint light that poured through the open doorway I knew it wasn't Danny.

"Shit," his father groaned, his head suddenly lowered again, his eyes downcast on the table. "Not now," he went on, dejectedly, "for Christ sakes it's Christmas Eve . . . "

"You're sixty days past due Mr. P.—you're running out of time and we're running out of charity . . . "

I knew the voice. I had heard it, it seemed, all my life. But right there, under the pantry, so still my knees had stiffened and ached under me, I could not place it.

"Another couple of a' weeks . . . " Danny's father began to protest, but the voice cut him off again.

"Who you kiddin' Mr. P.—you're outa free time—you start payin' today, I don't care if it's Christmas, Easter, or your wedding day—or your daughter's," the voice hesitated. "A bad debt makes *me* look bad, and I don't like it!"

I knew that voice like I know my own—but I couldn't place it. I strained my neck trying to see who it was, but there was no way.

"Here's a hundred, a down payment, the rest in a week . . . "
Mr. Polito threw a few bills across the table.

"A hundred won't get you shit. Five hundred, right now, at
this minute, will give you a week without pain."

"Well, that's it," Mr. Polito stood up and threw his arms open
as if inviting inspection of some sort. "There's no more . . . there's
no fucking more." He walked to the middle of the kitchen, looked
around as if lost, and threw his arms in the air:

"Do what you want—break up the place . . . break up every
dish in the house, go ahead." Then he looked straight at whoever
was standing there, raised his hands into two fists, and tried to collect himself into one last gutturally dignified statement: "Break my
nose," he said, touching his noise with his forefinger—in a way I
had always associated with Santa Claus, "if you can, you candy-
assed piece of manicured shit . . . "

It was at that point that I first caught glimpse of the intruder –
his black wool sleeve of his overcoat to be exact—as an arm thrust
forward, the lightning quick fist landing with the hollow smack of
flesh and bone against the sagging face of Danny's father. A gush of
blood spurt forth from his nose and splattered the white linoleum,
the table, and the metal ice of the hockey game.

Mr. Polito staggered back to the counter, his bright red hands
held to his face. The intruder stepped forward until he was a couple
of feet in front of the stunned and bleeding man—within easy
striking distance. In the dim, bland light of the kitchen, the circular
florescent light directly over his head like the halo of an unsuspecting, misguided angel, I recognized the culprit.

It was Carm Carlotta.

"You're gonna get hurt old man," he said, standing before Mr.
Polito, "all I want from you is the money you owe us—no fucking
lip, you understand . . . " Danny's father, his face a bloody mess,
broke into a grin and shook his head as he lay back against the
counter.

"Tell me Carlotta," he said, wiping the blood from his mouth,
"how does it feel to beat up an old man on Christmas Eve?" And
then, just as I thought the violence was over, he grabbed a coke

bottle from the counter and swung it wildly at Carm, who blocked it with his arm and ducked away from the shattering glass. Mr. Polito then drove himself forward, head first, into Carm's chest, leaving a splat of blood on his overcoat as they fell backward into the table onto the floor. They rolled over, and when Danny's father found himself on his knees above Carm who was still on his back, he lifted his fist, as if it were a rock, over his head.

But he never got the punch off. Carm, as quick as lightning, kicked him square in the chest and Mr. Polito tumbled backwards. Then the real beating began. Carm, jumping to his feet, pulled him to his feet and just as quickly drove his knee upward into Mr. Polito's groin. The groan was horrendous, and for the first time I had to close my eyes. The next time Carm kneed him, Mr. Polito fell forward onto the table, crushing the hockey game as he fell.

Danny's father looked almost unconscious at this point, and when Carm pulled him once more to his feet and cocked his arm as if to smash him again, I turned my head away. Already he had broken the old man's nose, probably a couple of ribs and who knows what else. But to my relief, he held back. Instead, he let Danny's father slide to the floor. Carm stood over him, taking a couple of deep breaths. He tried to brush himself off, but he was a mess, blood stains, dirt, and even pieces of the coke bottle sticking to the wool overcoat. He picked up a dish towel and wiped the blood from his knuckles.

"You sonofabitch," Carm uttered with anger toward the heap on the floor beside him, "you'll pay for this Polito, you'll fucking pay for this—I don't even give a shit about the money, *this*," he said, still brushing himself off, "*this* you'll pay for . . . "

Mr. Polito looked up at him, muttered something in his exhausted defiance, and passed out. Carm gathered up the bills that had made up the inadequate payment and stuffed them in his pocket. He kicked the ruined hockey game and stomped out the door.

I was still too frightened, too dumbfounded, to move. I wanted to disappear the way children do, by closing my eyes and being absolutely still. But there was another fear that brought me back to the reality of my young manhood. I couldn't bear seeing Danny discover his father like that. My god, I thought, as I made my way out of Danny's house and fled down the street to mine, if only they could have made their way to California when Mary Kay was a few months more innocent, less womanly. After all, what I always thought kept everyone in the neighborhood, whatever their dreams, their anger, was a genuine regard for one another. If I were Danny, the thought struck me, I'd kill Carm. I'd kill him.

* * *

I was still trembling twenty minutes later when I entered St Philips Church and sat alone in the back pew. I had a standing agreement with my mother—to go to confession on Christmas Eve and receive communion the next morning during Christmas mass.

Every year it became more difficult. What I could never quite pull off was finding decent words to describe my list of indecencies. A couple of years earlier, it was Billy ironically enough, the neighborhood all-American, who provided me with the key phrase to describe masturbation, feeling up Carol the Cootie in the back lot behind No. 25 School, or, worst of all, the onslaught of increasingly sexual fantasies that kept invading my everyday thoughts. "*Bad actions*," said Billy as we sat on the hill against the dead elm, "or bad thoughts—that'll do it; Father Phillips will know what you mean."

Well, apparently Father Phillips did know what I meant— because instead of letting me go on to lesser crimes of the soul, like swearing, stealing, and using god's name in vain, the whispering priest followed up my confession to "bad actions" with a series of intricate, graphic, embarrassing questions:

" . . . with a boy or a girl?" the elderly priest whispered.

"A girl," I answered, surprised at his apparent ignorance in these matters.

"Where?" he continued in his insistent whispers, "where did you touch her?"

"In the empty lot behind the school . . . "

"No, no . . . I mean *where*, which part of her body did you touch?" He still whispered, but he sounded a little annoyed or anxious.

When I didn't say anything, he repeated his question. It wasn't that I didn't want to confess—it's just that I couldn't utter any of the only words that came to my mind. How could I sit in that dark, pious booth and spit forth the words *tits*, or *boobs*, or *jugs*—or even *breasts* for that matter.

"Well . . . ?" It was obvious Father Phillips wanted an answer.

"Chest!" I spurted out, relieved to have found an accurate, legitimate word, "I touched her on the chest Father . . . "

But that was just the first of the lengthy line of embarrassing questions, which included—always in that whisper that gave confidentiality a universal quality, as if each secret utterance were being taped for a finale of a playback on the eve of that judgment day—questions such as:

How many times?

Did she touch you? Where?

How many times?

Did she make you come?

Did you touch yourself?

Where?

How many times?

And then, finally, the question to which your answer invalidates the whole procedure: "Will you do it again?"

"No father," I answered, wanting to get my ass out of that booth, "never."

I swore on that day never to bring up the subject of sex in a confessional booth again (and I didn't).

And on that Christmas Eve I didn't intend to change my policy—though it wasn't sex that was on my mind. I was still shaken of course by seeing Danny's dad beaten by Carm. It struck me as I made my way to the dark confessional booth, swept back the curtain, knelt, and placed my lips near the small screened opening where Father Phillips waited on the other side, that I was there to confess sins I could not yet fathom.

Could I say that I wasn't simply a thief, but a thief with a heart, and a charitable one at that? Could I say that my silence in the midst of physical violence was a virtuous kind of a well-meaning observer? Could I say that Leona's sentiments were more significant to me than Billy's death itself? Could I say that I stole my father's and my sister's words in the name of intelligence and not selfishness? I mumbled the opening prayer, "I confess Father, for I have sinned . . . "—a trick I learned as a youngster when I could not remember all of the words. I went through my meaningless list of god's offenses—the small, spiritual betrayals of a pedestrian existence. I estimated the number of times, expressed sincere regrets for my acts, and avoided the mention of sex altogether. I whispered that I was ready to accept the priest's penance, but thought to myself I did not even know the consequences of my young life. And then, as Father Phillips asked, as he always did, his parting question, it struck me that at the same time I was asking myself if I would never kneel in that confessional again . . .

"No," I answered, with my own reverent whisper, "never again."

* * *

We met, as we did every Christmas Eve, at 6 o'clock at Jim's *Superette & Delicatessen* on Bay Street across from Jack's *Mobil* station. Jim had opened his store more than a decade earlier. He was a friend of the neighborhood, seemingly intimate with everyone, apprised of everyone's health and habits. He extended credit readily, and seemed perfectly content to provide the staples of the neighborhood's grocery needs—bread, milk, potato chips, and six-packs of *Genesee Beer*—leaving the more intricate, more expensive items to the *A & P* in the nearby *Goodman Shopping Center*.

No sooner did I walk in and greet Cosmo and Danny then Jim, a calm, handsome man about fifty, asked us behind the meat counter. On the chopping block stood several bottles and glasses.

"Merry Christmas boys," said Jim as he poured three shots of anisette, "this will brighten your spirits."

We gulped them down, trying our hardest not to make a face. Jim laughed quietly as we did. It was a neighborhood tradition, not just to have a drink with Jim, but with anyone who owned a business in the neighborhood. By ten o'clock on Christmas Eve everyone was feeling good. We made our way to Jack's gas station; he was serving rum and cokes. Then we crossed the street and made our way to the corner of Baycliffe Drive for a quick visit—and a quick glass of homemade wine—to *Bernie's Market* and Bernie and his wife Rose, who slipped us each a *Snicker's* bar on our way out.

Back at the hill, we leaned against the elm and chased our drinks down with the *Snickers* bars. I didn't have much time as I had to meet Carm and the others at the *Bay & Goodman Grill* for the Sled Run to the orphanages.

"Well, another Christmas, huh creeps," said Cosmo, touching the candy bars together as if it were a toast. Danny seemed sullen, and of course I knew why. On the way to *Bernie's Market*, he asked me, in a kind of a whisper, what had become of me earlier that afternoon. I told him that I had snuck out as soon as I'd gotten a chance—when his old man visited the bathroom, I added, quixotically.

"Did you see anything?" he asked, tentatively, obviously not wanting to give anything away. I didn't know what to say.

"No, nothing," I replied. "Why, anything wrong?"

"No," said Danny as we entered Bernie's place, "nothing wrong." Cos looked at me and shrugged his shoulders. I would tell him later what had happened.

I was the first to reveal my gift. I pulled out my grandfather's jackknife from my coat pocket. Cosmo's eyes lit up.

"You sonofabitch Rosey," he said leaning over and hugging me as I handed it to him. "It's beautiful . . . just great," he added, removing his gloves and running his fingers along the red mahogany handle and then the extended blade.

"Merry Christmas Cos," I said, "you'll use it more than I will."

Cosmo reached into the bag he'd been carrying around all night. "This is for you Rosey." He handed me a cardboard covered forty-five record. I recognized it immediately. Jan and Dean's *Heart and Soul*. I had played it endlessly on Cosmo's record player at his house. No one else seemed to like it but me, and Danny and Cosmo teased me continually about my bad taste in music. I didn't care—I liked what I liked. A few years later, in the mid-sixties, I would be the only one to choose not *the Beatles* or *The Rolling Stones* as my favorite rock group, but *The Animals*, with *Freddy and The Dreamers* a not too distant second.

Danny seemed genuinely touched when I gave him the Cleveland Browns pennant with Otto Graham's autograph sprawled across it. "Gee Rosey, how could you give it away . . . I mean, this is special . . . " He seemed to have tears in his eyes, and when he handed me a small bag, he couldn't hold back the tears any longer.

"They were supposed to be a surprise . . . " he said, sniffing and trying to regain his composure.

I opened a small bag. I pulled out a bright red metal hockey figure. It was a Detroit Red Wing metal figure—my favorite team. Danny had found a set of them somewhere, and I could switch them with those of one of the teams that came with the hockey game. It was a marvelous present, I thought, forgetting for a moment the irony Danny was blurting out between his tears:

" . . . but the surprise is, the whole fucking game is ruined . . . " He put his arms around me. "I'm sorry Rosey . . . "

"What happened?" whispered Cosmo, who had no idea what was going on.

"Some things,' Danny, his head now against the elm, " . . . they came in and beat up my old man—some old gambling debts or something . . . " He pulled out a handkerchief and blew his nose. Getting a hold of himself, he turned to us and continued with one of those sad smiles one carries around forever in the involuntary file of memories.

" . . . and somebody must have stepped on it, fell on it or something—but anyhow, it's ruined, crushed to shit, I'm sorry Rosey."

"Hey Danny, that's okay, it's okay—as long as your dad's okay."

"Banged up—the bastards must have put a boot in his face from the looks of it, but he's okay . . . "

"Who did it?" asked Cosmo in his innocence.

"I don't know, he doesn't say." Then Danny looked at me. "Did you see anyone, anything, Rosey?"

"No," I lied again. "It must have happened after I snuck out."

"I'd kill the motherfuckers if I knew . . . "

"Easy Danny, easy . . . " I walked over and put my arm around him. Cosmo, instinctively, came over and did the same.

"Danny," I whispered now, my voice suddenly reverent, though I didn't know what I was about say. "Danny, why are we here tonight, the three of us?" Why are the three of us here, together, every Christmas Eve?"

Danny wiped his eyes. Cosmo squeezed Danny's shoulder, and, mockingly but lovingly, answered my question: "To get fucken' free drinks at Jim's, Jack's and Bernie's, right?" We laughed, and Danny wiped his eyes again. I had to wipe mine too.

"When we got a problem, we got each other, right. I mean for us Christmas isn't a special day by itself—it's the spirit we have for each other every day of the year—that's what's special. I mean how many other guys meet up the hill like this on Christmas Eve every year?"

"You fucking guys are the best," gushed Danny, kissing each of us on the cheek.

"Jesus," said Cosmo, "what two friends I have, a preacher and a fag!"

"No, I mean it," Danny remained serious, "I couldn't find better friends that you guys.'

"You're not bad yourself," I added

"You know," continued Danny, the look in his eyes a little distant now, as if we stood on that hill for a reason afterall, "You know, someday—I mean someday a long time from now, when who knows where we'll be or what we'll we doing—there's gonna be a Christmas Eve that comes along we're gonna leave everything and show up on the hill here—lean against this tree like I'm doin' now, and just wait for the other two to show up—and we'll be here, all of us, cause we'll know . . . "

We stood there for a moment, unable to say anything. The meaning of our friendship jelled in my mind that night, I could feel it. I could feel it as strongly that night as I would its absence in many nights to come.

"Here, I almost forgot," laughed Danny, breaking the spell. For you Cos, you goddamn pig you—Merry Christmas."

We spent the next few minutes passing around the pornographic photos Danny discovered in yet another of his father's dresser drawers—his gift for Cosmo. I left my two friends laughing on the hill under the huge snowflakes that had begun to fall. I had to meet Carm and the guys at the *Bay & Goodman Grill.* It was, of course, the night of Sled Run.

CHAPTER X

"Just about to leave without you Bright Boy," quipped Carm, then downing a shot at the bar. He wore a light blue suit that looked like it was made out of silk. His shirt was white as a bedsheet brought in from drying in the sun, the collar starched and perfectly folded over a read paisley tie. Thrown over the bar, I noticed a camel hair overcoat. The black one, I suddenly remembered, was stained with Mr. Polito's blood.

I tried to avoid looking right at Carm. Around him were the envoys of the evening—Bambi, his black hair slick with grease, black suit, black tie; Curley, with his drab brown sport jacket and a tan dress shirt with an open collar (I didn't think there was a shirt large enough that would button around his neck!); Little Christo looking chubby and happy as ever, smelling of *Jade East* aftershave, but already looking like he could use a quick shave.

Before I could mumble my way through an apology for being late, Carm reached out and, with his hand behind my neck, pulled me toward the bar.

"Come'ere Bright Boy, there's somebody I want you to meet."

Turning on the barstool next to Carm was an extremely good-looking young man with curly hair and the most handsome, however pronounced Italian nose I had ever seen. He had a warm, knowing smile, and his clothes looked very expensive (moreso than Carm's), topped off by a grey herring-bone overcoat and a white silk scarf. He reached out to shake my hand.

"This is Sammy C. Bright Boy. Sammy, Bright Boy here's our newest sled runner. Not much bulk, but a lot of brain," Carm laughed.

I shook his hand. We all knew about Sammy C. One day he'd run the whole show, maybe all of the Northeast I heard Johnny Pops say one night. I felt bad that my hand was so cold when I grasped his.

"So this is Bright Boy, eh, Carm," said Sammy C., lifting a small thin cigar out of his pocket, "a bouncer he'll never be," he laughed and the others laughed too. "Merry Christmas kid," he said looking at me. Then he pulled a ten dollar bill out of his pocket and placed it firmly in my hand; "Merry Christmas Bright Boy, thanks for helping out."

Just as we were going out the door Carm yelled over to Cookie, one of the bartenders. "What's that?" he asked, nodding over to the corner where something vaguely the shape of a Christmas tree was covered with big sheets of seasonal crepe paper.

"A surprise for later . . . when you get back. You'll see," said Cookie, cleaning a glass with a big smile, adding, "go gettum Santa . . ."

St. Joseph's Villa was our first stop. I drove in the Cadillac with Carm, Bambi, and Sammy C. It was the smoothest, quietest car I had ever ridden in—and I think Bambi, sitting with me in the back seat, was equally impressed. Behind us, carrying the load of presents as if it were a sleigh, were the others in the red van. We drove slowly, effortlessly, down the long driveway off St. Paul Street.

"Wait til you see these kids' faces," said Carm into the rearview mirror.

"Yea, it makes it all worthwhile," added Sammy C. as he pulled the Caddy into a parking spot of one of the houses, "if you know what I mean."

Curley pulled the van in next to us. We got out, but no one got out of the van. I felt a momentary relief that we wouldn't be filling it with loot that night, parked in the shadows of some warehouse parking lot.

"Wait about five minutes," said Sammy to Curley, "then start bringing the shit in."

The orphanage knew we were coming. We were met at the door by a grey-haired gentleman who apparently had something to do with running St. Joseph's. He called Sammy C. *Mr. Cardonelli*, and Carm *Mr. Carlotta*. I didn't know quite what to expect, but I was surprised at the peace and orderliness of the place. Several boys were sitting in the parlor we were led to—just sitting there, hands folded, ties against their collars, sweaters and sport jackets, each one standing and shaking our hands. A Christmas tree was decorated elegantly in the corner of the room, its lights twinkling on and off, and a star glittering at the very top. It was not what I had expected of an orphanage. A couple of boys, about my age, came in with a tray of cookies and cups and a silver pot filled with coffee. They set it on a cocktail table in the middle of a huge room. And just as Carm held his napkin under his chin and bit delicately into a frosted cookie the shape of a Christmas tree, a group of about ten boys marched in dressed in white choir gowns.

We sat through several carols, "White Christmas," "We Three Kings," "Oh Little Town of Bethlehem," and a snappy version of "Sleigh Ride." I watched Sammy C. and Carm sitting back, nodding with little grins on their faces expressing their approval. At the end of the medley we all applauded and the choir bowed and paraded out of the room. The worn, white and black sneakers sticking out from under the hems of their gowns was the only thing that seemed right to me. In contrast, Carm drinking a glass of milk did not seem real.

The gentleman with the white hair then stood up and introduced Sammy C. (as Mr. Cardonelli) and Carm (as Mr. Carlotta) to the boys in the room—who, some standing now, and others sitting on the floor, seemed to number forty or fifty. He thanked too the Italian-American League and the Italian-American citizens of Rochester for their charitable Christmas spirit. The orphans applauded politely. Sammy C. then stood up and, as if he were a politician making a campaign stop, made a few ingratiating remarks before holding up his hands and saying, "Let's get on with the gifts, hey guys."

Little Christo and Curley marched into the explosion of hollering, applause, and whistles, carrying groups of large, brightly colored packages. They set them in a huge pile in the center of the big parlor. I tried to remember what it was we had gathered so quickly and darkly during the our nightly runs through warehouses. But the green, red silver wrapping paper made them look so different, so legitimate I could not remember. I nodded my head, as if taking inventory, as each was opened. The boys were not thrilled with the complete set of *Wonder Books*, but they certainly let out an appreciative yell when the paper was yanked off the hockey games. I thought of the smashed one at Danny's house, and remembered Carm, sitting there now so respectable, showing one of the boys how a ratchet worked from the unwrapped tool box . . . remembered him lifting his knee solidly into Danny's helpless dad a few hours earlier.

The kids seemed to love the baseball gloves, *Wilsons* and *Mac-Gregors*, as well as the footballs and baseball bats. A couple of boys took the fishing poles and flyrods into the corner to examine them. Others seemed fascinated with the *Scrabble* sets and *Monopoly* games. I was surprised to see so many admire the shirts and pants assortment which we lifted one night from *Robert Halls* on Monroe Avenue, the same place my mom and dad shopped with me for our school clothes. And when they opened the box of baseball jackets, I thought there was going to be a fight right there in the parlor—but the grey-haired man quickly went over, whispered sternly in a few ears, and made the boys place them neatly in piles next to the Christmas tree.

Someone came in the room and whispered in Sammy C.'s ear.

"Mr. Pops?" I heard him repeat the name, obviously not understanding something. Carm leaned over with a puzzled look on his face, but before either of them could ask what was going on, none other than Johnny Pops, dressed in a plaid sport coat and a thick, brown tie, appeared from the hallway. He was all smiles and waved to us from the entranceway. Carm raised his arm weakly, and gave him a half-hearted wave back.

"What's this about?" asked Sammy C.

Carm shrugged his shoulders. Johnny disappeared for a moment, then entered the room again, this time carrying a large, apparently heavy box wrapped in glittering silver paper. He placed it near the tree and motioned for a couple of the orphans to open it. Two boys came up tentatively and poked at the box, pulling on the bow until it unraveled.

"Come on, open it," laughed Johnny Pops, seemingly as anxious as anyone for the gift to be opened.

Then they tore at it, the paper shreds, the cardboard box yanked open. On the side of the box I saw *RCA 19*, and before it dawned on me what it was, the two boys pulled out as portable television set! The rest of the kids let out a few gasps and then spontaneously began applauding. "Plug it in," someone yelled, and someone did. A light appeared in the center of the picture tube and then grew, brightened, and formed crystal clear images of Robert Young sitting at a kitchen table talking in austere sincerity to Budd and Kathy. Johnny stood there beaming, though I'm sure the irony escaped him.

"I'll be a sonofabitch," I heard Carm say under his breath. Sammy C. just looked at Carm and smiled, as if to say *so what*.

"The warehouse!" exclaimed Carm, to no one in particular.

"What?" said Sammy C.. Bambi walked over and knelt on one knee next to the others.

"The electronics warehouse—on Culver Road. That night we ran into my brother," Carm explained, then turning to Bambi— "the night that cop killed the fucking reindeer . . . So that's what Pops was doing there!"

Johnny whispered to one of the orphans who motioned to several others. In another minute, they were carrying three more identically wrapped boxes into the room. "One for each dormitory," exclaimed Johnny, all smiles. The older grey-haired man who had met us at the door whispered to Johnny and shook his hand for what seemed like five minutes. One by one the orphans opened the boxes. Each was identical: a brand new 19-inch portable television set. One by one the boys made their way up to Johnny and thanked him.

"Sonofabitch," muttered Carm, shaking his head.

"What's the difference," said the self-assured Sammy C., "it's all in the same family, right . . . "

I watched the orphan kids surround Johnny Pops. The glow on his face seemed to light up the room at least as much as the Christmas tree lights of the avalanche of glittering paper scattered over the room. It struck me that, at Christmas, even the small-time punk couldn't be denied in the charitable heart of this petty thievery—and for a moment or so as the kids surrounded the four T.V.'s and played with the volume and adjusted the brightness, Johnny stood in the spiritual spotlight of the picture tubes' blue glow—his private sled run the most fulfilling ride of all. Carm still sat there shaking his head, as if accepting the fact that there was no justice in the world, even in the midst of the kindest gestures. Nasty, small-mined, bully, dead rat smelling Johnny; for the moment I was pulling for the bastard.

The scene repeated itself that night at all our Sled Runs. At the *Hillside Children's Center* off Monroe Avenue, and at the *Monroe County Home for Children* on Henrietta Road. Each time Johnny showed up, gaudy, awkward but joyous with four brand new television sets for each place. At the last orphanage, Carm and even Sammy C. shook Johnny's hand and thanked him. "We all do what we can Bright Boy," he said, beaming and actually patting me on the head.

On the way to the *Bay & Goodman Grill* for our Christmas Eve celebration—where we met every year and even the younger kids were allowed a beer or two—Carm turned to me in the back seat of Sammy C.'s Cadillac. "I think there's an extra hockey game Bright Boy—you want it?"

For a moment, a chill passed through me. Perhaps he knew that I knew the other one was smashed when he beat up Danny's father. Then it occurred to me that maybe he knew I had been there witnessing it all.

"No thanks Carm," I heard myself say.

"He's waiting for a television set," laughed Bambi, and then the others laughed with him.

They did not know what was waiting for us at the *Bay & Goodman*.

* * *

Sammy C. let us off in front. He thanked us and took off. It had stopped snowing and the winter sky was so clear there was a star shining for every one of God's wanderers.

Inside the celebration had begun. Johnny Pops had beaten us back and was ordering a round for everyone when we walked in. Danny and Cosmo came over and shook my hand, congratulating me on my first Sled Run. They were both a little giddy and I could smell beer on their breath. Dutch came over with Cosmo's brother, Mike, their arms around each other's shoulders, already intoxicated.

"You little shiz better wash what yer drinkin', "slurred Mike, leaning forward and burping ceremoniously in his brother's face.

Just then Johnny Pops stood on a barstool next to the bar and clanked a better stein against a half-empty pitcher. He motioned to Cookie the bartender who turned the jukebox music down from behind the bar.

"Let's make a toast," said Johnny, still elated by his unsuspected role in Sled Run. "I just want all of you to know—all of you who didn't get a chance to go to the orphanages tonight—that tonight's Sled Run was, well . . . it was the best ever . . . right Carm?" He nodded over to Carm, then me . . . "Right Bambi . . . huh Rosey?"

We all nodded, though I heard Carm, who was standing behind me, mutter, "milk it, milk it you dumb fuck."

"I wish you coulda seen those kids' faces, right guys? I mean after tonight they know us Italians is good people who have a heart at Christmas. They loved their gifts guys. They're gonna be happy little muthers playin' their games and wearin' their new clothes— and," Johnny's face brightened even more—"watchin' their new T.V.'s . . . "

The word must've gotten around because everyone started applauding and whistling when he said that. He put up his hands as if to acknowledge and quiet the applause.

"Well now," he continued, and then made an exaggerated nod to Cookie who made his way to the end of the bar. "Well now, I think we've all been good boys, isn't that right?" His remark was followed by a bellow of comments, moans and cat calls.

"So," Johnny went on, his hands still pushing against the air, "Johnny has gotten something for everyone this year. Cookie . . . " He motioned again to the bartender who stood by the Christmas tree where the glittering sheets covered an enormous pile. Cookie pulled on the sheets and under them were the silver-wrapped packages, all the same, all, it struck me immediately, the size of the boxes Johnny had given the orphans.

"Shit, I don't believe this!" Carm exclaimed behind me.

"There's a name on each package—one for everyone," said the beaming Johnny Pops.

Mike was the first one to find his package. Johnny warned everyone that the packages were extremely fragile. Mike looked stunned, as if he had mistakenly opened something, when he discovered it was a television set.

"Holy shit Johnny, are you kiddin'," shouted Curley, finding his and opening it as easily as a cigarette pack.

"They're all the same," exclaimed Johnny, walking among us, shaking hands and wishing everyone a Merry Christmas, "televisions for everyone . . . they're all the same, genuine 19 inch RCA's, brand new models . . . "

Carm had planned a surprise for us too—freshly carved reindeer meat brought out on trays with Italian bread and hot sauce. But it was, of course, anticlimactic. The salty tasting meat only made everyone more thirsty, more drunk, and more insistent on expressing boisterous gratitude to Johnny Pops.

Danny seemed, at least for the moment, to have gotten over his father's beating. He kept looking at me and Cos with the silliest of drunken looks: "Can you believe it, a fucken' T.V. for everyone!"

But not for me.

"I just don't want it, that's all—we got one, okay." I said, having refused the package marked Rosey.

"Sell it for god's sake," said Cosmo.

And finally Johnny Pops sunk back into his usual character, looking suddenly like his small, resentful, angry self: "What's the matter Rosey, it ain't good enough for ya . . . "

When we left the *Bay & Goodman* a cop pulled up and, seeing us carrying television sets, jumped out of his car. But when he saw that just everyone coming out of the door was carrying one, he brushed back his policeman's cap, shook his head and said, "Merry

Christmas," and got back into his patrol car and drove off. On the way home Danny and Cosmo struggled down Bay Street with their televisions. My arms felt incredibly light, free. We heard a loud, piercing crash behind us, more like a gun exploding. Dutch, who had managed to get pretty drunk, had dropped his television in the middle of Bay Street. Everyone laughed so hard they had to put down their televisions for a while.

Underneath the streetlamp in front of Danny's house we said goodnight. Cosmo and Danny were still asking me why I had refused the television, and I said, truthfully, that I didn't know why I did, except that it felt right at the time. I watched Danny struggle up the front porch steps. I wondered if the new T.V. would make his father feel any better.

"Poor Danny," said Cosmo, "finding his dad beat-up like that, huh . . . "

"Yea," I said, "that's rough."

"Isn't Johnny Pops something," he said, patting the RCA box in his arms. "I mean after I stuffed his car with the rats and all."

"Yea, something else."

"You shoulda taken one Rosey, you know—it wouldna done ya no harm."

"No," I said, turning toward my house, feeling suddenly exhausted, but somehow a little better, almost happy. "No, probably no harm at all."

PART THREE

*

Christmas Morning

CHAPTER XI

I awoke with Judy tugging at my shoulders, shoving the morning paper in my face.

"Wake up," she shouted, "wake up you flaming plagiarist you—you're famous." Lonnie stood behind her, already a picture of the quiet, serene woman she would become.

I tried to focus on the newspaper. I was feeling the effects of the beer from the night before at the *Bay & Goodman*. For a few seconds my dream flashed one last time through my mind: a room full of wounded, bandaged, bloodied, black and blue orphans staring hypnotically into the blinding light of a television.

"First page Rosey—look at it!" exclaimed Lonnie.

I re-opened my eyes. Sure enough, there I was. On the front page of the Christmas morning *Democrat & Chronicle*. Sitting at a table with my hands against the keys of Judy's Smith Corona portable typewriter—the way the reporter had me pose.

"My god!" I said, amazed to be on the front page, "I don't even know how to type!"

"You don't write poetry either you asshole," said my sister Judy in her sarcastic manner, "but there's *your* poem in black and white."

"My god . . . " I managed to utter.

"A hundred thousand people," continued Judy, "will start their Christmas morning by reading your poem . . . "

"Dad's poem," I corrected her.

"Well, nobody will know that, will they?"

"So what," Lonnie came to my sleepy defense, "what's the difference—if they knew dad wrote it, it wouldn't be there. They'd run a photo of that ugly tree at Midtown Plaza instead."

"Where's dad?" I asked.

"Downstairs, having breakfast," replied Judy, suddenly jumping off my bed and heading down the stairs. "Wait til you see him! We're all going to mass today—including dad, remember?"

Lonnie added, "Even she's going—the neighborhood communist anarchist atheist!"

I threw on my robe and started downstairs. Before I reached the kitchen I noticed another oddity on the front page of the newspaper. At the bottom of the page was a photo of a reindeer, and next to it the headline *Missing Reindeer Joins Santa at North Pole*. It was a humorous account of what happened to the reindeer that escaped somewhere in Rochester during *Sibley's* promotion and could never be found. I laughed to myself, still tasting the salty venison on my breath from the previous night.

I had to look twice when I walked into the kitchen. My dad was standing there holding the coffee pot above my mother's cup. He looked dashing. A three-piece brown striped suit, white shirt with a tan and white striped tie, and white and black winged tip shoes. His white hair seemed equally as elegant as his clothes, and his smile when he saw me was as warm, knowing, and sincere as any, I was sure, that Old Saint Nick might muster. My mother too looked beautiful. Her striking black hair set off by the soft violet dress and simple string of pearls around her neck.

"Shit," I blurted out, "you guys look . . . well, terrific."

"Right from the poet's mouth," Judy wise-cracked.

On the table were stacked a bunch of newspapers. Then my dad saw me glance at them, he said "your mother made me go out and buy all of them at the superette—I don't know who she is prouder of," he added, "her good-looking son on the front page here, or her talented husband who's the author of this poem that everyone's calling about."

"We got six calls already," my mother blushed forth—"everyone loves it; they can't believe you wrote it . . . "

That got a big laugh out of all of us.

"Well you couldn't have written it without me, huh Rosey," said my father, coming over and putting his arm around me, " and I couldn't have published it without you."

"Anyhow, nothing . . . " my father started to say, but I stopped him, because I knew what was coming.

" . . . is what it seems," I finished the phrase for him, and he smiled and shook his head at himself, a little embarrassed at his predictability.

As I downed a cup of coffee, I read again the Christmas poem on the front page:

Thaw: The Christmas Poem

Only the wings of
The angel remain,
Two drifts of snow.
How slowly
They float through the earth . . .

I'm no angel, That's for sure.
My anger forms on the window like frost.
It is frost.
In its intricate design I scrape
My initials, primitive claim
To my art.

And what else can I claim?
A job, a used car,
The promise of television?
Even the moonlight seems frozen.
My eyes are two small torches
Blazing at the window.
From a distance
I'm sure someone sees them as
Signs of peace and goodwill . . .

The icicle grows.

Every year my thoughts turn
To water.
I think, always,
This is the last season.
Even the light
Will have to bend though me . . .

And then such warmth.

"It's beautiful . . . a beautiful poem dad," I heard myself whisper after reading it through a couple of times. But when I looked up, no one was there except Judy, who turned to me from the sink with tears in her eyes.

"He's upstairs," she sniffed, wiping her eyes, "he wants to look good for this, this perverse duty you're making him go through . . . "

"What do you mean?" I asked, defensively, and then adding, confused by her tears, "what's wrong Judy, why are you crying?"

"Oh, what would you understand?" she half shouted, half cried.

"Try me," I said, and trying to lighten her mood and holding the newspaper up to her I added, "I'm a poet, remember?"

"Rosey, you ungrateful, spoiled, mothball-minded sonofabitch . . . " She sat across from me at the table. "Did you read that poem?"

"Read it? Who me, the author . . . "

"Cut the shit, you dumbbell!" she burst out at me. "Didn't you see dad's face this morning?"

"He looked great, that suit . . . "

"Not his clothes you ass—him, his face when he read that poem over. That shoulda been his photo, his name under the poem. That's talent—it wasn't meant to win a contest for adolescents. Oh, he laughs and pats you on the back and goes along with it because he loves you and he'd do anything to inspire you. But he might as well be wearing that suit this morning for the same reason he always does—to go to a funeral. Because if you look at his face, dear old Bright Boy, you'd see he's acknowledging the death of his talent and his love for words—which no one ever gave him the time of the day for."

She wiped her eyes again, and then reached over and grabbed my hand, warmly. "And now you're asking him to go to church, as if to give thanks to God for all of it . . . Jesus, Rosey."

The phone rang twice more as I dressed for church. I heard my mother's laughter as she explained that "Rosey got his talent from his dad of course . . . "

I met my father on the stairway. He straightened my tie and pushed my hair back away from my eyes.

"Dad, you don't have to go to church on account of me."

He smiled and put his arm around me. "Rosey, you know that I wouldn't go if I didn't want to—you know me better than that."

I looked at him. For a man who in Judy's eyes was acknowledging some deaths of sorts he sure looked good—that sparkle deep in his eyes.

"It'll be fun for me, educational even—I want to see if there's a difference between my faith and that of your criminal friends," he laughed. But I think he was half serious.

"My, my, look at my handsome men," said my mother, looking up from the bottom of the stairway. Together, we made our way down the stairs, our awkward steps graced by the light and love of my mother's earthly admiration.

* * *

It was as bright a Christmas morning as I could remember, the sun reflecting off everything with a symbolic brilliance. In front of St. Philips a few teenagers lingered, looking equally restless and awkward in their cheap baggy suits.

Right in front of the church, in a no parking zone, was Carm Carlotta's sparkling candy-apple red Mercury—top down! Danny and Cosmo were there, waiting for me as usual. They were surprised to see my father walking behind us.

"What's your father doing here?" asked Danny, solemnly, as if something might be wrong.

"Just a promise, it's nothing," I whispered, shrugging off any explanation.

"Aren't you going to sit with your father?" my mother asked. Before I could answer, my father gestured me to sit with my friends. Judy gave me a dirty look. Lonnie looked preoccupied, as if she were looking for someone.

"Nice poem Rosey, first fucking page," Cosmo congratulated me.

"I'll say," added Danny, "my father gave me hell because I didn't write a poem—thanks a lot Rosey," and then he laughed that infectious laugh and we put our arms on each other's shoulders and walked into the church. We ended up sitting in a pew directly in front of my family, and I felt a little relieved, for my mother's sake, being close to my father. It seemed that an unusual number of people tried to catch my eye that morning. Being on the front page of the newspaper in our neighborhood was, of course, a very big deal. But I was shocked when Father Phillips began his sermon that Christmas morning by alluding to—by actually quoting from!—my poem . . . that is, my father's poem. Then everyone seemed to turn around and strain their necks to get a glimpse of me. I turned around and my father smiled at me, looking proud as punch. My mother reached over and patted my shoulder. Judy stuck out her tongue.

Cosmo and Danny poked me with their elbows. And kid as they would about it, which of course was a certainty, I could see a genuine pride in their faces. This would be a secret, I decided then, assuming that even Jesus Christ would understand, that I would keep for a long time. Father Phillips's sermon was about the warmth of spirit even during the worst of times. He said something about balancing hope with good will, and how every soul had its season and so forth. I guess that's what my dad had in mind thirty years earlier when he'd written the poem. The priest quoted the last lines from the clipped newspaper article, which he held in his hands.

> Even the light
> Will have to bend through me . . .
> And then, such warmth.

"Thanks Rosey," he added, extending a personal gratification in the middle of the sermon, adding, "we'll look for more of your wise words in the days to come." I put my head down, turning red from shame, not humility. The whole damn congregation was eyeing me. My simple Catholic guilt added a new partner—Fraudulence. *Shit*, I uttered, not quite as softly as I meant to. A few people turned around in front of us, and Danny and Cosmo began to chuckle. I turned around and my mother was beet red. Did she hear me? Or was she feeling the same guilt? Afterall, it was my mother who snuck me into the closet and showed me my dad's poems in the first place.

I passed up communion. Never again, I said to myself. I didn't join in on any of the hymns or Christmas carols either. And yet I heard right behind me a voice rising beautifully, apart from the others. It was my father. He sang with the same spirit as he did singing *Sunny Side of the Street*, or *Nightrider in the Sky*. I thought he'd spend his hour in church hiding in the shadows of the neighborhood faith. But he was having fun. And he was eloquent to boot.

"What's with your dad?" asked Cosmo again.

I shrugged my shoulders and rolled my eyes. Nothing was what it seemed, I told myself.

My bewilderment grew with the collection. Passing one basket in the main aisle was Carm, looking as slick as ever in a light blue silk suit. And directly across from him, passing the other basket as they made their way down the aisle in unison, was Danny's father, looking contrastingly stout in his dark brown suit, and wearing his wounds like combat commendations—his nose swollen, a cut on his cheek, and a purplish black eye. I watched them both as they approached us, working their way up from the altar. For the moment it struck me that there was some important distinction to be made—as whether to deposit your envelope into one man's basket or the other. I felt an incredible rush of charity on one hand, but when Carm passed the basket down our row—he was on our side of the aisle—I instinctively placed my envelope containing a dollar into my pocket instead. A moment later, I felt my mother poke me in the back. She didn't look too happy. No doubt she had seen me pocket the envelope. My father was busy writing something on the weekly handout.

On our way out as the mass ended, several people congratulated me and shook my hand. Near the entrance of the church as the lines from the three aisles merged on their way out, I saw Leona a few feet ahead of me. I kept looking at her until our eyes met. She looked beautiful as ever, especially as the sun passed through the stained-glass above the doorway and touched her hair. I didn't know what I expected of that moment, but when she simply nodded and turned back to Barbara and her girl friends, I felt, foolishly I realized, abandoned.

Everyone gathered in front of the church to exchange Christmas greetings. Dutch came up to us with his black eye (that Danny had given him for his remark about his sister), and jokingly asked Danny if he'd given one to his old man as well. What Danny did give to his father for Christmas was the television from Johnny Pops. "That pleased him," said Danny, making light of his father's appearance, "almost as much as the ice-pack for his eye."

Suddenly, although the sun blazed, big flakes of snow began falling. Bambi, wearing his usual black suit and black tie to match his jet-black hair—looking more like a funeral director than a future loan-shark—came up to us with Johnny Pops, who obviously was still enjoying his charitable good-standing of the night before:

"You sure you don't want that television Bright Boy—nothing like T.V. to get ideas for your new poems."

I shook my head, and he shook my hand. I hoped his Christmas high would carry him through a few more days. Even Danny and Cosmo were kinder toward him—no one mentioning the smell of dead rats.

Leaning on the railing by the front steps was Little Christo, looking as chubby, dark-faced and happy as ever, holding hands with Danny's sister, Mary Kay, who, despite her fall into a mortal existence, still was the most beautiful girl in the neighborhood— perhaps, it struck me as she shook hands with and hugged several people who were congratulating the couple . . . perhaps even more beautiful because she was living not just for one more human being inside of her, but for many of us who could suddenly and honestly merge such beauty with the reality of a pedestrian life.

As I stood there on the front lawn in front of St. Phillip Neri Church, there in the snow-flaked sunshine of a hundred acquaintances, the thought came to me that I might never own a brand new Mercury convertible, or hear my father sing another Christmas carol, or be given credit for a single written word ever again. But nothing, I found myself repeating, was what it seemed. The bells rang around us, signaling a spirit made precious by a simple acknowledgement. I saw Lonnie, so poised, so accepting of her blossoming womanhood, shyly, discreetly giving a little wave to a young man I didn't recognize. Judy, for all her cynical determinations, laughing like a kid with her schoolfriends. My mother, forever attentive to the aesthetics of detail, straightening a corsage on the lapel of a neighbor's coat.

And my father, standing next to me, nodding to everyone—Carm, Father Philips, and even Danny's father, shaking his hand as well. He was radiant, looking more content, I remember saying to myself, than an atheist could ever be.

Going down the front steps, Leona walked up to Carm's convertible with one of her friends. She leaned over and picked a few snowflakes off the front leather seat. Carm seemed to appear from nowhere, opening the passenger door, and in an exaggerated gentleman's bow, swept his arm forward, as if offering her not simply a ride, but a grand entrance into a lifetime's journey. Leona laughed, and she and Barbara stepped back on the sidewalk. Nothing was what it seemed. I realized that I might never take or even touch Leona's hand again. But it seemed all right. I glanced up at my father who seemed to be staring out at nothing, everything. I watched Leona throw her head back and deliver her smile to no one in particular. No, I might never touch her lips again. But it was all right.

I knew that it would be all right.

finis

ABOUT THE AUTHOR

 Known as one of our country's most accomplished multi-genre writers, ROSS TALARICO has published, among his numerous publications, three classic books in three different genres. His non-fiction work, *Spreading The Word: Poetry and the Survival of Community in America* (Duke University Press), examined the potential enrichment of writers discovering their social roles and the link between democracy and the self-expression of ordinary people; it won *The Shaughnessy Prize* from The Modern Language Association for outstanding book of the year on literature and writing. Another classic was his book of narratives (memoirs) based on oral histories of elderly Americans, adapted for the stage and re-defining the genre—*Hearts and Times: The Literature of Memory* (Chicago Academy Publishers) . . . which caused Studs Terkel to state "Ross Talarico has a rare talent; he captures the inner thoughts of ordinary people and reveals their extraordinary visions." And in 2008 he published one of the great long poems of the century, *The Reptilian Interludes* (Bordighera Press), an epic which explores—through a father seeing his family evolve and devolve in a transmission from humanistic to technological existence —"a new understanding of what it means to be human in a world where the Gods of Dante and Milton have been replaced by the Gods of science and technology;" critic Frederick Turner remarked, "Ross Talarico has set himself to repair the breach in our sensibility and to recover the lost territories and languages of natural understanding."

And now, with *Sled Run*, perhaps we are seeing another classic, this time fiction, unfold before our eyes—a heart-warming Christmas tale about getting ahead in blue-collar America, a story filled with hope, crime, good intentions and difficult choices.

Talarico's writings have appeared in hundreds of publications, including *The Atlantic, Poetry, The Nation, The North American Review, Arts and Letters*, and *The American Poetry Review*. He is a nationally recognized educator, Professor at Springfield College, and lives in San Diego along with his children.

Author photo: Amanda Kriska

VIA FOLIOS

A refereed book series dedicated to the culture of Italian Americans in North America.

FRED MISURELLA, *Only Sons*, Vol. 79, Fiction, $17
FRANK LENTRICCHIA, *The Portable Lentricchia*, Vol. 78, Fiction, $17
RICHARD VETERE, *The Other Colors in a Snow Storm*, Vol. 77, Poetry, $10
GARIBALDI LAPOLLA, *Fire in the Flesh*, Vol. 76, Fiction, $25
GEORGE GUIDA, *The Pope Stories*, Vol. 75, Fiction, $15
ROBERT VISCUSI, *Ellis Island*, Vol. 74, Poetry, $28
ELENA GIANINI BELOTTI, *The Bitter Taste of Strangers Bread*, Vol. 73, Fiction, $24
PINO APRILE, *Terroni*, Vol. 72, Italian American Studies, $20
EMANUEL DI PASQUALE, *Harvest*, Vol. 71, Poetry, $10
ROBERT ZWEIG, *Return to Naples*, Vol. 70, Memoir, $16
AIROS & CAPPELLI, *Guido*, Vol. 69, Italian American Studies, $12
FRED GARDAPHÉ, *Moustache Pete is Dead! Long Live Moustache Pete!*, Vol. 67, Literature/Oral History, $12
PAOLO RUFFILLI, *Dark Room/Camera oscura*, Vol. 66, Poetry, $11
HELEN BAROLINI, *Crossing the Alps*, Vol. 65, Fiction, $14
COSMO FERRARA, *Profiles of Italian Americans*, Vol. 64, Italian American, $16
GIL FAGIANI, *Chianti in Connecticut*, Vol. 63, Poetry, $10
BASSETTI & D'ACQUINO, *Italic Lessons*, Vol. 62, Italian American Studies, $10
CAVALIERI & PASCARELLI, Eds., *The Poet's Cookbook*, Vol. 61, Poetry/Recipes, $12
EMANUEL DI PASQUALE, *Siciliana*, Vol. 60, Poetry, $8
NATALIA COSTA, Ed., *Bufalini*, Vol. 59, Poetry
RICHARD VETERE, *Baroque*, Vol. 58, Fiction
LEWIS TURCO, *La Famiglia/The Family*, Vol. 57, Memoir, $15
NICK JAMES MILETI, *The Unscrupulous*, Vol. 56, Humanities, $20
BASSETTI, ACCOLLA, D'AQUINO, *Italici: An Encounter with Piero Bassetti*, Vol. 55, Italian Studies, $8
GIOSE RIMANELLI, *The Three-legged One*, Vol. 54, Fiction, $15
CHARLES KLOPP, *Bele Antiche Stòrie*, Vol. 53, Criticism, $25
JOSEPH RICAPITO, *Second Wave*, Vol. 52, Poetry, $12
GARY MORMINO, *Italians in Florida*, Vol. 51, History, $15
GIANFRANCO ANGELUCCI, *Federico F.*, Vol. 50, Fiction, $15
ANTHONY VALERIO, *The Little Sailor*, Vol. 49, Memoir, $9
ROSS TALARICO, *The Reptilian Interludes*, Vol. 48, Poetry, $15
RACHEL GUIDO DE VRIES, *Teeny Tiny Tino's Fishing Story*, Vol. 47, Children's Literature, $6
EMANUEL DI PASQUALE, *Writing Anew*, Vol. 46, Poetry, $15
MARIA FAMÀ, *Looking For Cover*, Vol. 45, Poetry, $12
ANTHONY VALERIO, *Toni Cade Bambara's One Sicilian Night*, Vol. 44, Poetry, $10
EMANUEL CARNEVALI, Dennis Barone, Ed., *Furnished Rooms*, Vol. 43, Poetry, $14
BRENT ADKINS, et al., Ed., *Shifting Borders, Negotiating Places*, Vol. 42, Proceedings, $18
GEORGE GUIDA, *Low Italian*, Vol. 41, Poetry, $11
GARDAPHÈ, GIORDANO, TAMBURRI, *Introducing Italian Americana*, Vol. 40, Italian American Studies, $10
DANIELA GIOSEFFI, *Blood Autumn/Autunno di sangue*, Vol. 39, Poetry, $15/$25

Published by Bordighera, Inc., an independently owned not-for-profit scholarly organization that has no legal affiliation with the University of Central Florida and the John D. Calandra Italian American Institute.

FRED MISURELLA, *Lies to Live by*, Vol. 38, Stories, $15

STEVEN BELLUSCIO, *Constructing a Bibliography*, Vol. 37, Italian Americana, $15

ANTHONY J. TAMBURRI, Ed., *Italian Cultural Studies 2002*, Vol. 36, Essays, $18

BEA TUSIANI, *con amore*, Vol. 35, Memoir, $19

FLAVIA BRIZIO-SKOV, Ed., *Reconstructing Societies in the Aftermath of War*, Vol. 34, History, $30

TAMBURRI, et al., Eds., *Italian Cultural Studies 2001*, Vol. 33, Essays, $18

ELIZABETH G. MESSINA, Ed., *In Our Own Voices*, Vol. 32, Italian American Studies, $25

STANISLAO G. PUGLIESE, *Desperate Inscriptions*, Vol. 31, History, $12

HOSTERT & TAMBURRI, Eds., *Screening Ethnicity*, Vol. 30, Italian American Culture, $25

G. PARATI & B. LAWTON, Eds., *Italian Cultural Studies*, Vol. 29, Essays, $18

HELEN BAROLINI, *More Italian Hours*, Vol. 28, Fiction, $16

FRANCO NASI, Ed., *Intorno alla Via Emilia*, Vol. 27, Culture, $16

ARTHUR L. CLEMENTS, *The Book of Madness & Love*, Vol. 26, Poetry, $10

JOHN CASEY, et al., *Imagining Humanity*, Vol. 25, Interdisciplinary Studies, $18

ROBERT LIMA, *Sardinia/Sardegna*, Vol. 24, Poetry, $10

DANIELA GIOSEFFI, *Going On*, Vol. 23, Poetry, $10

ROSS TALARICO, *The Journey Home*, Vol. 22, Poetry, $12

EMANUEL DI PASQUALE, *The Silver Lake Love Poems*, Vol. 21, Poetry, $7

JOSEPH TUSIANI, *Ethnicity*, Vol. 20, Poetry, $12

JENNIFER LAGIER, *Second Class Citizen*, Vol. 19, Poetry, $8

FELIX STEFANILE, *The Country of Absence*, Vol. 18, Poetry, $9

PHILIP CANNISTRARO, *Blackshirts*, Vol. 17, History, $12

LUIGI RUSTICHELLI, Ed., *Seminario sul racconto*, Vol. 16, Narrative, $10

LEWIS TURCO, *Shaking the Family Tree*, Vol. 15, Memoirs, $9

LUIGI RUSTICHELLI, Ed., *Seminario sulla drammaturgia*, Vol. 14, Theater/Essays, $10

FRED GARDAPHÈ, *Moustache Pete is Dead! Long Live Moustache Pete!*, Vol. 13, Oral Literature, $10

JONE GAILLARD CORSI, *Il libretto d'autore*, 1860–1930, Vol. 12, Criticism, $17

HELEN BAROLINI, *Chiaroscuro: Essays of Identity*, Vol. 11, Essays, $15

PICARAZZI & FEINSTEIN, Eds., *An African Harlequin in Milan*, Vol. 10, Theater/Essays, $15

JOSEPH RICAPITO, *Florentine Streets & Other Poems*, Vol. 9, Poetry, $9

FRED MISURELLA, *Short Time*, Vol. 8, Novella, $7

NED CONDINI, *Quartettsatz*, Vol. 7, Poetry, $7

ANTHONY TAMBURRI, Ed., *Fuori: Essays by Italian/American Lesbians and Gays*, Vol. 6, Essays, $10

ANTONIO GRAMSCI, P. Verdicchio, Trans. & Intro. , *The Southern Question*, Vol. 5, Social Criticism, $5

DANIELA GIOSEFFI, *Word Wounds & Water Flowers*, Vol. 4, Poetry, $8

WILEY FEINSTEIN, *Humility's Deceit: Calvino Reading Ariosto Reading Calvino*, Vol. 3, Criticism, $10

PAOLO A. GIORDANO, Ed., *Joseph Tusiani: Poet, Translator, Humanist*, Vol. 2, Criticism, $25

ROBERT VISCUSI, *Oration Upon the Most Recent Death of Christopher Columbus*, Vol. 1, Poetry, $3

CPSIA information can be obtained
at www.ICGtesting.com
Printed in the USA
FSOW02n0125200516
20579FS